# One Last Dance

## A Hopes Crest Romance

Book 2

Laura Hayes

Copyright © 2018 Laura Hayes

All rights reserved.

This book is a work of fiction. Names, characters, businesses, places, events and incidents are either the products of the author's imagination or used in a fictitious manner. Any resemblance to actual persons, living or dead, or actual events is purely coincidental.

All verses included in this text are from the New King James Version translation.

# Hopes Crest Romance Series

Starting Over

One Last Dance

The Billionaire's Bet

# *Chapter One*

Four Years Ago

Jenny Hunter took a deep breath and headed back to stand under the artificial lights which hung high above the gym floor. It was the night of her senior prom, and though it should have been one of the happiest moments of her life, it had proven to be not so.

As the head cheerleader who was dating the star baseball player, everyone had the impression that her life was great. The fact was, the opposite was true. For the last two months, Jenny and her boyfriend had been arguing nonstop, and it was clear those arguments would not end anytime soon.

The music seemed to have gone silent as Mark Davis, Jenny's boyfriend and prom date, stood waiting for her in the middle of the gym floor. He looked so handsome in his tuxedo with his dark hair combed over in unruly, yet lovely, waves.

"Have I told you how beautiful you look tonight?" Mark said as he took her hand in his and placed the other hand on her waist.

Jenny and her mother had taken a trip to Denver a little over a month earlier to select that particular prom dress, and Jenny had to admit, she did look great in it.

It was not that she was snobby or self-centered, but she was also a realist; the way the other boys turned to look at her appreciatively as she walked by was enough to tell her that she looked good. "Blue suits you so well. It matches your eyes," he added.

"You're too sweet, Mark," Jenny said as the music slowed. The DJ got on the mic and said a few words as an old tune from the 1950s played over the speakers.

Nearly ninety students would graduate this year from Hopes Crest High School, one of the largest classes to date, and every single senior seemed to fill the cordoned off dance floor.

It would have been entertaining to watch the other dancers as some stepped on toes, their faces tomato red with embarrassment, while others swayed stiffly back and forth as if the idea of such an intimate situation was foreign to them. And it probably was; they were teenagers after all. However, Jenny and Mark were among those who felt comfortable with each other, and so they managed to avoid one another's feet and kept time with the music. It was as if they had been made for each other.

"I wish you would reconsider," he whispered in her ear. She looked up at him, but before she could respond he added, "We graduate Friday and Monday morning we can leave in my car. The future is ours and you know I will take care of you." His voice was now pleading. "You know I love you, don't you?"

Jenny smiled. She knew he loved her, and she loved him. She loved him more than anything in this world, but the thought of running off to California was more than she could bear. And besides, they were not married and she didn't want to live with him, even in separate bedrooms, without a ring on her finger. It was not what she had planned for her life.

The song came to an end and the DJ's voice came over the speakers. "All right, ladies and gentlemen, one last slow song for the evening. Enjoy."

Jenny laid her head against Mark's chest and his strong arms pulled her in closer. As the soft music played, her mind began to wander. What if she took off with him? They could get married in Las Vegas on the way.

But what about her parents? And though she loved Mark, she was not sure if she was ready to marry him just yet. It was unfair of him to expect her to drop her entire life and run off with him like this.

As the song ended, Jenny gazed up at Mark just as he leaned in to kiss her. It was soft, sensual—and over rather quickly as Katie Baxter, Jenny's best friend, came rushing up with Chris, her date.

"Are you guys ready for the after-party?" Katie asked, the excitement clear in her voice.

Jenny took Mark's hand in hers and shot him a quick glance. "We'll be there in a bit," she said.

Katie leaned in and kissed Jenny's cheek. "Good," she replied. "We'll see you in a few." Then she and Chris walked off together.

"Jenny, let's forget the party," Mark said beseechingly. "Let's head back to my place; my parents won't be back until tomorrow, so we'll have the place to ourselves."

Jenny squeezed his hand and began walking toward the exit. "No," she replied in a soft but firm voice. "I can't do that, Mark, and you know it."

She knew that he would never overstep his bounds or do anything inappropriate, but she was worried about how it would look. Plus, she would have to lie to her parents.

Once outside, people were laughing and talking as they got into limos, pickup trucks, and cars, most driven by the students but others by parents who had either refused to allow their children to borrow the family car or the youngsters who were not old enough to drive.

When they arrived at Mark's truck, he turned to her, his eyes pleading. "Seriously, Katie's party is going to be lame. Besides, we need some alone time to talk about California. Hollywood is calling, you know?" He was smiling down at her, but she felt her frustration grow. Could not a single night pass without them arguing? Apparently not.

"Mark, I can't go to California. It pains me to say it, but I can't. You just have to be okay with that."

"Fine," he said stiffly, his voice clearly showing his irritation. "Then at least come with me so we can talk everything out."

"Don't do this to me, please," Jenny said. The fact she was upset he would be leaving was enough without the added pressure to go to his house, a parent-free house at that.

Mark took a step back. "Do this to you?" he said, his eyebrows raised. "Do you realize that within a year I'm going to be a huge Hollywood star? Women are going to be throwing themselves at me.

I'll be rich, richer than anyone in town, and I want you by my side when that happens."

Jenny had been fighting back tears all night, but now one escaped. "I will support you," she said quietly, "but I'll be doing it from here." She reached out and took his hand in her own. "I can't go with you, but I will be waiting here for you when, and if, you return."

He yanked his hand from hers. "There's no point then," he snapped. "I'm not going to have a girlfriend a thousand miles away. You know long-distance relationships never work. Either you come with me now, or we can just call it quits."

"Are you serious?" she asked, her heart sinking. "You're going to break up with me because I won't run off and marry you?"

"What do you expect me to do?" he demanded. "Wait?"

"Well, yes," she replied, though her tone sounded uncertain.

"For what? What is going to change in the next six months, or the next year for that matter?"

"We can work on us, Mark," she said. "We've been fighting way too much lately. And besides that, you're running off to become some big star. You threw away your scholarship and you're risking everything."

His laugh was humorless as he leaned against his truck, his arms crossed over his chest. She recognized the look on his face. He was angry. "Yeah, I know," he said disdainfully. "I'm supposed to go to college like everyone else in town and then maybe go pro, right? Well, let me ask you this. What're you going to do with your life? Stay in Hope?"

Jenny nodded. "Yes, for the time being anyway. I feel like I belong here. I'm not saying you shouldn't go to Hollywood and chase your dreams, but don't break up with me just because I don't want to go with you."

"Then come with me."

Jenny sighed. This was going nowhere. She went to explain to him that the break would do them good after so many months of arguing, but before she could speak, he placed his hands on her shoulders.

"I'm going places in this world," he said. "It's what I want and I'm sorry you don't want to be a part of it." He paused and looked down at her for a moment and then added, "Goodbye, Jenny."

He walked around to the driver's side and slid behind the steering wheel without another word. Tears streamed down her face as he turned the key and the truck engine rumbled.

"Mark?" she cried, but he ignored her. A moment later, the truck began to pull away from her, and she banged her fist on the passenger side window. "Don't you dare leave me!" she screamed. "I love you!"

He shook his head without looking at her, and Jenny sobbed as the taillights disappeared into the night.

What was meant to be a special night, her senior prom, had turned into a disaster, and now she was left alone in the middle of the empty parking lot of Hopes Crest High School. Pulling out her cell phone, she dialed Katie's number.

## *Chapter Two*

Present Day

Jenny Hunter let out a calming breath as she glanced at the small silver cross that was on her desk. It was a sign of not only her faith but also something to turn to when she felt like pulling her hair out. Like now.

It was the second week in August, and school would not be starting for another two weeks. However, the sports programs would begin before the school year commenced, and as the high school cheerleader and girls' sports coach for the coming year, she was feeling a bit overwhelmed. Parents had already called to ask about their children's placement on a team that had yet to be formed.

Most of the girls who wished to try out for the cheerleading squad were already gathered in small groups in the gym, the excitement in their voices Jenny could hear even down the short hall and through the closed door. Dealing with a bunch of teenage girls was not an easy task but at least this year she would have help.

A knock came to the door and Jenny pulled her long brunette hair back over her shoulders. "It's open," she called out and then smiled as Molly Hanson, her new assistant coach, came walking into the office and closed the door behind her. She had met the woman at church just over a month ago, and since she was a single mom, she had expressed how much she needed a job.

"Hey, Coach," Molly said in her happy-go-lucky voice. "I'm ready for my first day."

Though the woman was twelve years older than Jenny at the age of thirty-four, she dressed like she was seventeen with numerous silver earrings dangling from her ears, several rings on her fingers, tattoos running down her arms and a t-shirt that screamed rock star instead of coach.

"Yeah, you are," Jenny said with a smile as she walked over and gave Molly a hug. "Are you nervous?" She pulled out the chair in front of the desk and Molly took a seat.

"No, not really," Molly replied, moving her short dark hair behind her ear. "I just want to make a good impression is all."

Jenny nodded and returned to her seat behind the desk. Reaching to her side, she grabbed the three shirts she had ordered for Molly. "Here're your shirts for now," she said as she handed them to Molly. "Come winter, I'll have a jacket made for you, as well." She glanced at the multitude of rings on the woman's fingers. "And I'd suggest losing those rings; they might just get in the way."

Molly stretched her fingers out in front of her. "You're right," she said, clearly embarrassed. "I'm sorry, I didn't even think of that." She pulled the rings off her fingers and dropped them into her purse. The poor woman was shaking visibly, and Jenny reached across the desk and grabbed one of her hands.

"Listen, your job is secure," she said in a clear, firm voice. "I'm not planning on firing you, especially over some rings." Though Jenny had only known Molly a short time, the two had hit it off at once and had even gone as far as to hang out a few times, so she hoped the woman could hear the sincerity in her voice. "Just relax and try to enjoy it because, trust me, these teenage girls are going to be driving you wild soon enough."

Molly let out a breath as if she had been holding it for a while. "Thanks," she replied with a relieved smile. "I feel better now."

Jenny gave her hand a squeeze. "You got it," she said. "Go ahead and head to the locker room and change. If you want, give me your purse and I'll lock it in my desk for you."

"Yeah, I appreciate it," Molly replied. "I don't even know why I bothered to bring it."

Jenny laughed. The sounds of shouting and laughter got louder as Molly opened the door. "Don't worry, it took me forever to realize I didn't need to bring my purse to practice. You'll get used to it."

Molly gave Jenny a grateful smile and left the office with one of the shirts, the door shutting to muffle out the girls once again.

Jenny shook her head as she headed out of the office. She had no doubt that Molly would adjust, just as Jenny had when she first started. Once she had closed and locked the door behind her, she stopped to study the group of girls she would be coaching this year and stifled a laugh.

Several of the returning cheerleaders were already practicing old cheers from the previous year, their voices loud and boisterous, just as they had been taught. Several new faces watched in clear fascination, their toes tapping in time to the cheer beats and their arms shifting stiffly as if attempting to copy the moves. A third group sat clumped together, mirrors out as they applied makeup.

"Lord, give me strength," Jenny whispered.

However, rather than calling the girls together, she walked over to a large glass trophy case that held several photos and awards from previous years. A smile crossed her lips as she studied a photo of her cheer squad four years prior, although the time seemed much longer than that.

Then her eyes fell on a plaque and a picture of the baseball team from that same year.

For the first time in Hopes Crest High's ninety-year history, that team had gone all the way to the state championship, led by none other than their power hitting outfielder Mark Davis, whose individual photo had been placed beside the baseball he had hit to make that winning home run. He wore the same wicked grin on his handsome face as he always did, and seeing it made her smile.

She had been so in love with him back then. They had been the perfect couple, and Mark had been offered a full-ride scholarship and the chance to play pro ball one day. Yet, he had thrown it all away—the scholarship, the pro-ball opportunity, and Jenny, all in one fell swoop.

Without warning, Jenny's mind returned to prom night and her fists beating against the window as she cried for him to stay. She shook her head, trying to erase the memories from her mind, though they were ingrained in her heart and therefore so much more difficult to get rid of.

"Hey, how do I look?" Molly asked, breaking Jenny from her thoughts.

Jenny smiled as she gave Molly a once-over. The blue shirt with the white Hopes Crest insignia and the sword beneath it was positioned over her left breast. When Molly turned around, the word "Coach" was spelled out in white on the back.

"You look great," Jenny replied. "Now, like me, you need one more thing to make you an official coach." She reached into her pocket and pulled out a whistle that hung from a blue piece of string.

"Aww, I might cry," Molly said as she took it from her. "Thank you."

"You're most welcome," Jenny said.

The sound of heels clicking on the wooden floor made them both turn, and Linda Miller, Hopes Crest High principal, came walking up. She walked with a confidence that Jenny could only envy, and though she was fair when it came to her leadership with students and staff, she was also known to be more than a bit mean.

"Ladies," Linda said in her stern, crisp voice, "I just wanted to let you know that Arthur has decided, at the last minute, that he's not coming back to coach this year." It was clear she was not too happy that the man had inconvenienced her, as if it was some sort of decision made to attack her personally. "I do have an interview lined up today, and I ask that you welcome to our school whomever I hire."

"We most certainly will Linda," Jenny said. As if she was the type to be rude to anyone, especially someone new. Then she gave Molly a gentle elbow.

"I know I will," Molly replied quickly.

Linda gave a small snort. "Very well," she said. "I will see you later." She turned and then stopped and glanced over her shoulder. "Oh, and I do hope your softball team does better than last year's." With that, she clicked back across the gym and out the heavy doors.

Once the doors slammed behind the principal, Jenny rolled her eyes and then winked at Molly. "Come on, Coach," she said. "The exciting world of girls' sports awaits."

***

Ten girls who wanted to participate in cheerleading this year were lined up side by side along one of the white painted lines on the gym floor. Jenny let out a sigh, her hands on her hips as she sized each of them up. There were a few familiar faces from the previous year, but a couple of new ones stared back at her nervously.

Molly's daughter Emma stood beside her best friend Sam, a girl who had gone through some struggles over the past year.

"Well, girls," Jenny said, "the good news is that everyone gets to make the team no matter what." This brought on a round of applause and cheers. "The bad news is that there is only one spot for captain, so over the next few weeks, both Coach Molly and I will be watching you. Keep in mind it's not only the effort you put on the field, but off-field, as well. How do you treat your fellow teammates? Do you help another girl who might be struggling on a cheer? Or do you watch her fail? The choice is yours." She turned and gave Molly a nod.

Two days earlier, Jenny had prepped Molly for her first day, and now was the time to see if the woman was up to the task.

"We run a tight ship here," Molly stated in a firm voice. "Any mouthing off or back talk will result with me getting rough with you." She raised a fist and slammed it into her other hand, which brought on a few snickers from the girls. "Ladies, I'm joking, of course," she continued with a smile. "We're here for you and want you to know you can come to us at any time for any reason."

Jenny smiled and turned back to the girls. "Any questions?"

A senior raised her hand.

"Brianna?"

"My mom told me that, when she used to cheer here, Kayla was made captain because everyone thought she was pretty. Is that true?"

Sam's face reddened and Jenny groaned.

"No, of course that's not true," Jenny replied. "No matter how you think things were done in the past, which I can say with certainty was not as you think, we run things fairly. From what I understand, Kayla was an all-around great student and representative of our school, so I'm sure she earned her position as captain. Now, are there any more questions?" The girls shook their heads. Jenny was glad a fight had not broken out. "All right, ladies, we have some time before the boys come in and take over the gym. Mary," she nodded to another girl who had been last year's captain, "get the girls started on stretches."

"You got it," Mary said with a smile. She stepped forward and turned to face the rest of the team. "Okay, girls, follow my lead."

Soon, the group was busy with their warmups, with a few of the girls groaning because more than likely they had not kept active over the summer.

Jenny leaned in close to Molly. "Let them warm up a bit more and then we can start going over some basics," she said in a low voice.

Then a group of boys came into the gym yelling. There was nearly a dozen of them, and before she knew it, basketballs were flying everywhere.

"What's going on?" Molly asked. "I thought we had the gym until two."

Jenny pursed her lips. "We do," she replied through a clenched jaw. She walked over to Kyle, the previous year's star guard. "Kyle, what are you guys doing here?" she demanded. "We still have the gym for another hour."

"Sorry, Coach Jenny," Kyle replied, "but our coach told us to come on out. He's back near your office if you want to talk to him."

Jenny thanked him. It was not the boy's fault his coach had no clue what he was doing. She motioned to Molly that she would be right back and she made a beeline to the office door. Whoever this new guy was, he was going to learn that she ran the show around here.

## *Chapter Three*

Mark Davis pulled his truck into an empty parking space at Hopes Crest High School and turned off the engine. The silence that followed made his ears ring, and he leaned his head back into the seat and closed his eyes. It was coming up to noon and, in ten minutes, he would have an interview for a coaching position as well as a position as a part-time physical education teacher.

Having just returned to town two days earlier, Mark was thankful that his mother was friends with Linda Miller, the principal, and she had helped set up this interview. He opened his eyes and allowed his gaze to wander over to the sports field, and memories of him playing in the state championship flashed through his mind.

It was the bottom of the ninth, two out and two on base. They were behind by one. He could feel his heart race as the first pitch flew past him as it always did, the umpire calling a strike. He never took the first pitch. The next pitch, however, was the one people would talk about forever, because that baseball, according to some, never landed.

That should have been one of the happiest moments of his life. His girlfriend Jenny had rushed onto the field and he picked her up and swung her around in his arms. Not only had she been proud of him, but so had his father.

Yet, no matter how happy his play had made them, despite how proud he might have felt, he still had been sad overall. He did not mind playing baseball, but he did not love it. No, what he really loved had been the theater and the idea of one day becoming a star.

Shaking the memories from his thoughts, he got out of the truck and looked up at the tall light post beside him. It had been just over four years that he had parked here in this exact same spot in this very truck. Jenny had looked like a million dollars in her blue dress. With her long brown hair and beautiful blue eyes, he had often wondered what she had ever seen in him.

Then he had gotten the wild idea of making it big in Hollywood, and he must have known early on that she would refuse to go with him because he began pushing her away.

Yes, he had loved her, but he still broke her heart right under the very light post under which he now stood, and he had no excuse he could make to justify what he had done other than a wish to follow his dreams.

He pushed back the anger that threatened to overtake him and reached inside the driver's side door to pull out a small flask. He had been trying to cut back, but sometimes he needed something to take the edge off rather than dealing with his emotions.

He took a sip and then another, just in case the first did not kick in right away. In the past, he would pray in times of trouble, but somehow over the last four years, he had drifted away from prayer—and from God. Not that he did not say the odd prayer here and there, but the few times he did were only said half-heartedly.

Only a few cars sat in the parking lot as he made his way to the front doors of the school. He went straight to the office where Carol, the secretary who had worked there even when he had attended, sat behind the same desk wearing the same short hairdo she had before.

When she saw him, she jumped from her chair and rushed around the long counter. "Oh, my Lord, if it isn't Mark Davis!" she said. "Oh, honey, welcome back to Hopes Crest." She gave him a tight bear hug.

Mark laughed. "Hey, Carol," he squeaked. "It's good to see you." Relief that he could breathe once again washed over him as she released the hug. "How have you been?"

She wiped at her eye and smiled. "I'm well, thank you," she replied. She took each of his hands in hers and looked him up and down. "My, it's so good to see you. To have a hometown hero back in Hopes Crest…Oh, we are so lucky."

Mark smiled politely but did not wish to stand there listening to anyone praise him. He had turned out to be a failure in life, and he could not see why anyone else could see him as anything else.

Carol leaned in conspiratorially. "Just between us," she whispered as her eyes darted around the empty office, "I know Mrs. Miller still thinks you're the greatest student to ever walk through those doors. I know you're going to get the job." She giggled and then returned to the seat behind her desk and flicked a thumb behind her. "Mrs. Miller's office is still in the back. You remember, don't you?"

Mark nodded. He did remember it all too well, having been sent a few times for misbehaving in class.

However, like Carol, Mrs. Miller thought Mark was better than the average students and so his punishments were always light. Mark thanked Carol and headed down the short hallway to find the door to the principal's office already open.

"Mark," Mrs. Miller called out as she came around her desk to greet him, "I am so happy to see you."

Although she had always been known for her sternness, she had always been nice to him, which brought on a bout of teasing from the other students, mostly boys, who claimed she must have had a crush on him. However, he knew better; she was close friends with his mother, and that was the real reason he got preferential treatment.

And the interview.

"Have a seat," Mrs. Miller said, indicating a chair in front of her desk as she returned to her own chair. "Tell me about Hollywood."

He wrung his hands as he tried to figure out how to tell someone he was a failure. "Well, it went well overall," he replied. What he said was not an outright lie, but it was not all truth either. "I was in a few commercials, had some walk-on roles, and even shot a pilot. Nothing fancy."

She smiled appreciatively. "You did a great job selling that hamburger," she said as though he had won a Nobel Peace Prize or something.

He wanted to change the subject, so he cleared his throat and gave his best smile. "So, this coaching and teaching job. What do you need from me?"

"Well," Mrs. Miller replied, "I know, you don't want to coach baseball; I get it, but I still don't understand why." She shook her head. "But your mom said I wasn't supposed to mention it, so I won't. What I'd like is our hometown hero to coach our boys' basketball and also run a few of the boys' gym classes. Would you be interested?"

Mark nodded. "That'd be great," he replied. "Basketball practice starts in a week, correct?"

She nodded. "Are you sure you don't want to get involved with baseball? I think you'd do such a great job as head coach."

"Thanks, but I think I'm done with baseball for a while," he replied. In his mind that had meant permanently.

This had been a subject of contention between Mark and his father when his mother offered to speak with Mrs. Miller; his father felt he should use his already honed skills to help the baseball team and he wanted nothing at all to do with the sport. Basketball, however, gave him the chance to do something different, and he looked forward to it.

Mrs. Miller shrugged. "Very well, then," she replied, though her disappointment was clear. "But if you change your mind, let me know. You know I give my favorite student whatever he wants."

He shifted uncomfortably in his chair. Oh, how he knew. All through his high school years, he had been favored by everyone in Hopes Crest.

Mrs. Miller handed him a packet of papers. "Fill these out and bring them back to me later," she said.

"Thank you, Mrs. Miller," Mark said. "I really appreciate you giving me this opportunity."

She laughed. "You're a little old to be calling me Mrs. Miller, don't you think?" she asked, a twinkle in her eye. "You'll be a faculty member now, so you should just call me Linda from now on."

He was not sure how he felt about that, but then again, he was an adult now. Maybe this would be a way of feeling like he had finally grown up. Yes, the idea was appealing. "Okay," he replied happily, "Linda."

"Excellent. Now, let me show you to your office." She stood up and led him out of the room.

This had been the easiest interview he had ever done in his life and he almost laughed. "You're going to have to share, but I think you'll be happy when you find out who you're going to share it with."

***

After unlocking the door, Mark put the office key in his pocket and flipped on the switch on the wall. The halogen lights buzzed to life and he took a look around the tiny office. A large metal desk sat in the middle of the room, the owner clearly a very organized person; everything seemed to have its place.

He smiled as he picked up the silver cross that rested on a small stand in the corner. His mind went back to when he used to attend church in Hopes Crest. He actually hadn't minded going, and it also gave him another chance to see Jenny.

He returned the cross to the stand and rubbed his temples. Finding out that Jenny had been the cheerleading coach came as no surprise to him; she had loved it when she was a student here, and he knew she was probably loved by all of the girls. It was inevitable.

A small student desk sat in a corner and a two-drawer filing cabinet sat in another. On the wall behind the desk was a large whiteboard calendar and times had already been written on different dates, color-coded based on whether the dates indicated practices or games, if he guessed correctly. She had not changed much in the past four years, that much was evident.

He turned and walked back out of the office and over to a large trophy case that sat just outside the door. His eyes immediately fell on a photo of Jenny smiling at the camera, pom-poms in her hand and a leg bent up so her foot rested on her knee. She had always been beautiful, and Mark had gone through many a sleepless night with regrets for leaving her the way he had.

However, that was a long time ago. There was no reason to cry over spilled milk. But there were ways to clean it up, and he already had plans as to how that would happen.

Not only would he take this year's basketball team to the state championships, but he would also have Jenny on his arm once again by the time they held up the trophy.

Granted, things had not gone as planned over the past four years. In fact, they had gone horribly wrong. But now was his chance to prove himself once again, and Jenny was a part of that plan.

"Hey, are you the coach?" a young man perhaps sixteen years old said, breaking Mark from his thoughts.

"I sure am," Mark replied with a wide smile. "My name is Coach Mark." He offered his hand and the boy took it and gave it a firm shake.

"Wow, I know you," the boy said with a gasp. "Well, of you, anyway. My dad said you're the best ballplayer to ever come out of the school."

Mark laughed. "Maybe," he replied. "What can I do for you?"

"Well, me and some of the guys are already here and we wanted to start early. Can we head to the gym and warm up a bit?"

Mark nodded. "Sure, go ahead," he replied, glad to see at least a few on his team were excited to get started. "I'll be there in a few."

The boy thanked him and ran off.

Turning back to the trophy case, Mark looked once again at the photo of Jenny. How he had loved her back then, and truth be told, he still did. Although he had dated a few women while he was in California, he never did find anyone to get serious with. He often found himself wondering about Jenny and what she was doing, even when he was on a date.

He heard the sounds of hurried footsteps and then that sweet angelic voice he had only dreamed of for the past four years; a voice he had missed terribly.

"Hey, we have the gym until two," Jenny said.

Mark turned to face her and his heart skipped a beat. Yes, she was four years older, but she looked even more beautiful than he had ever seen her before. Her hair was still long and was pulled back into a ponytail. Her dark eyes were still the same, as was her face, which was even more stunning than he remembered.

"Mark?" she said in a stunned voice as she halted in mid-step.

"Hello, Jenny. It's been a while."

## *Chapter Four*

The air around Jenny congealed and her heart and feet stopped at the same time. Before her, not ten feet away, stood her ex-boyfriend, Mark Davis.

The world began to spin as old feelings of anger and longing made their way to the surface.

"Hello, Jenny. It's been a while."

"What are you doing here?" she demanded, though her words sounded as if they came from some far-off place, behind a wall of cotton balls.

He was still as handsome as ever with his wavy dark hair and brown eyes, but that smile was what sent shivers down her spine.

Yet, despite the attraction she obviously still had for him, the memories of what he had done to her fought their way to the top of the mess that was her mind, and anger broke through. How could he simply show up here, today?

"I came back to Hope just a few days ago," Mark replied. "My mom talked to Principal Miller and got me a job here. I guess we're both coaches now."

He took a step forward with that huge grin on his face she remembered all too well, but Jenny stood her ground.

"You can't work here," she said, crossing her arms over her chest. "There's too much bad blood between us and I think it would be best if you found somewhere else to work."

He shook his head, though his smile remained as he took yet another step forward. Now he stood just inches from her and it took every ounce of willpower to keep from taking a step back.

"Jenny," he said in that same silky-smooth voice she remembered all those years ago; that same voice that haunted her dreams for so long after he left, "we had something special, and I know we still do." He placed a hand on her arm. "I know you still care about me, just like I care about you."

Jenny stared down at his hand and the smoothness she heard in his voice suddenly sounded more like oil than silk. How dare he touch her! She pushed his hand away and took a step back.

"No, Mark," she spat, "we are over. You can't just walk in here and act like nothing happened, that everything is fine."

Her attempt at keeping her tone level was failing completely, but if she did not make that attempt, she would have been shouting at him.

"Listen, maybe we can go to dinner later," he said. "Catch up on old times?"

She shook her head and then turned away as Molly came around the corner.

"Hey, Coach," Molly said, "what should I do about the boys?"

Mark glanced over his shoulder and said, "Tell them Coach Mark said to head out to the hoops on the blacktop. I'll be right there."

He turned back and gave Jenny another grin, as if he had done something heroic for her. He was still such a jerk.

"Thanks," Molly said. "Oh, I'm Molly, by the way." She stuck out her hand. "Nice to meet you."

She must have finally felt the tension in the air because she shook Mark's hand quickly and then left without another word, though she did glance back at the pair before she was out of sight.

"Listen closely, Mark," Jenny said, seething, "I don't care how much people around here worship you. Not at all. We are professional colleagues and nothing more. Do you understand?"

That irritating grin spread wider across his face and he nodded. "Got it, Coach."

"Good."

What she had to do next chafed her to no end, but it would have to be done sometime.

"Now, let me show you the office."

She reluctantly led him into the room behind her, wishing there was some other place they could put him. A janitorial closet would work just fine as far as she was concerned. She pointed to a small student desk in the corner. "That's yours."

"What?" Mark asked in surprise. "That's like a time-out desk. There's no way I'm taking that."

She ignored his complaints and went over to the filing cabinet and opened the top drawer. Inside were two men's shirts still in their plastic wrappings, and she took them out and handed them to him.

"This is your uniform. We have the gym until two for the next few weeks. After school starts, Monday through Friday we split it after school until five. Any questions?"

He stood gaping at her for a minute before he replied, "I'm only doing the basketball thing because I'm keeping away from baseball, though I was offered the job, of course."

Jenny shook her head and went over to sit in the seat behind the desk. Of course, he would not be coaching baseball. Why would he take an opportunity when it was handed to him, but that meant that later their teams would be traveling together, and she really did not look forward to that. Any time spent with this man was too much time.

Mark must have been thinking of their shared travels as well because he said, "Do you remember when we went to Denver for the playoffs?" He set the shirts on the small desk next to him and sat on the corner of it. Jenny, however, chose to ignore him, hoping he would take it as a clue to leave. He didn't. "Me and you in the back seat of the bus. There was so much in our future back then."

Jenny could not keep the cynical laugh inside. "You mean your future. It was all about your games, your popularity and what you wanted in life. I remember a four-hour bus ride with you talking nonstop about California." She looked him up and down with disgust. "Apparently that didn't work out too well, did it, Champ?"

Pain flickered in his eyes for a moment and she regretted her words immediately. Even after all he had done to her, she truly did not want to hurt him.

"I'm sorry," she said as she lowered her gaze to her hands, which she had clasped on the desk. "That was uncalled for."

"Hey, it's okay," he replied. "Listen, I want to talk to you at some point. There's a lot I want to share with you." His voice became pleading. "Come on, surely we can go to dinner or something."

Jenny bit at her lip. If she agreed, she wanted to be clear that it would not be a date. In fact, it was probably best if she kept away altogether. However, like she learned in church from a recent sermon, it was best to get rid of old grudges.

"Okay," she replied. "We can go to dinner tomorrow night after practice."

This made Mark smile. "Great! It's a date, then."

She whipped her head up to glare at him. "No, Mark," she said firmly.

This was exactly what she had feared and she had to make him understand that there was no chance they would be getting back together. Her heart could not take it again. "It's not a date. It's two people meeting up to talk about old times and to catch up. After dinner, we go our separate ways."

"Fair enough. Not a date." He walked over and picked up the silver cross. "I remember giving you this. I'm glad you still have it." She said nothing as he placed it back on the stand and walked to the door. Then he paused and looked back at her. "Jenny?"

"Yes?"

"For what it's worth, I'm sorry. For everything. Thanks again for agreeing to go with me." A moment later, he was gone, his footsteps echoing in the hallway. Jenny was shocked how humble he sounded. But was it an act?

The silver cross caught Jenny's attention and she walked over and ran her hand along the cool metal. She remembered Mark giving it to her like it was yesterday.

"It's a symbol of strength and love," he had said. "Look at it whenever you need hope."

Yes, it was a symbol of those things—strength, love, and hope—and right now, more than ever, she needed strength.

She wiped the lone tear that rolled down her cheek. Enough tears for that man had fallen to last her a lifetime; she was not going to waste another minute on them.

A light knock came to the door, and she wiped quickly at her face to be sure it was dry. When she turned, Denise, one of sophomore members, stood shyly at the door. Cheerleading had been made for girls like Denise; it brought out something from within this girl every time she participated and she went from a quiet and timid tenth-grader to a bright and vibrant teenager.

"Coach?" the girl asked in her quiet voice. "Do you have a minute?"

"Of course. Come on in."

Denise stepped inside the office and closed the door behind her. "I…I wasn't able to get the shoes required for the uniform," she said in a voice barely above a whisper.

"Is that so?" Jenny asked carefully. From what Jenny understood, Denise lived with her grandmother after her parents landed themselves in jail for drug charges, and the girl did relatively well, but Jenny figured money was pretty tight in that household. She felt her heart go out the young woman. "You know, I can help out with that…"

Denise cut her off. "No, Coach, I don't want charity." Her timidness suddenly disappeared and her voice was firm and brooked no argument.

"No, I suppose you don't," Jenny said as she walked around the desk and sat on the corner of it. "But what I was going to say was that I need someone to stay after and help put away the mats and help with the general clean up. Would you be interested in doing that? In return, I'll buy you your shoes and after each practice, I'll subtract a little from what you owe. That way you have your shoes right now, which you need, and you will be earning them yourself. Just call it taking it out on credit, only I will be the creditor."

Denise considered this for a moment and then nodded. "Yeah, I think that would work. Thanks, Coach."

Jenny smiled. "Anytime," she replied.

The girl gave her a quick wave and then left the room, and soon Jenny followed, her mind still reeling after seeing Mark. For a moment she considered he had talked her into the dinner, pulling a fast one on her. But a smile came to her face as she shook it off. No, those games were far behind her. She would go to dinner and let him know where he stood, which was far away, like he had always been.

***

Jenny leaned back into the couch and let out a heavy sigh. Katie, who was not only her best friend but also her roommate, sat beside her, her mouth hanging open as Jenny told her about her day.

"That's just crazy," Katie said once Jenny finished with her story. "I mean, it's been over four years and out of the blue he shows up like that? Just…wow." She shook her head in astonishment. "And you have to work with him? Do you think you can handle that?"

Jenny nodded, though she wondered the same thing herself. "It's crazy, yes, but it's like he's the same Mark but different. It's hard to explain, but he seems…I don't know, humble maybe?" Katie raised a single eyebrow.

"Let me explain. At first he was the old Mark and it drove me crazy. Then it was like a switch went off and he became this different person. I mean, he did apologize to me in the end, something he would never have done before."

Katie laughed. "Oh, come on. Mr. Hometown hero humble? Honey, that boy doesn't know the meaning of the word. Never has, never will."

Jenny turned toward her friend. "You're right about that, but that's not what I'm worried about. What about going to dinner tomorrow with him? Do you think it was a mistake to accept?"

Katie reached out and took Jenny's hand. "I think it's a great idea, actually," she replied in a quiet tone. Jenny was surprised her friend would agree. "Let's be honest here. You have a lot of hurt stored up inside, right?"

"Yes, that's true. I've never had that closure with him and I figured this was the best chance to do that." Despite how painful it was, she could not keep her mind from returning to prom night, and the memories made her clench her fist. Maybe she had not completely forgiven him after all if just the thought of that night made her so angry. Perhaps she had simply kept herself so busy since he left, she never took the time to consider forgiving him.

"I think you're hurt and angry and have a lot to say, even if you believe you don't," Katie said. "And by telling him how you feel, it will make you feel so much better."

"You're right." This was why Katie had always been her best friend; the woman knew her better than anyone else and always gave the best advice.

"You bet I'm right," Katie said with a single quick nod. She let out a heavy sigh. "Okay, I'm heading to bed; I have to open the store tomorrow. Julie's doing inventory for the next couple of days, and I told her I'd help her out." Julie Carter was the owner of Galaxy Video where Katie worked. "Are we still on for a movie on Saturday night?"

"Yep," Jenny replied. "I'll see you tomorrow after dinner with Mark."

Katie reached over and hugged Jenny. "I want to know everything," she demanded in Jenny's ear. Then she stood up and headed down the hallway toward her bedroom.

Jenny finished off the last of her Coke and set the empty can on the coffee table before heading to bed herself. Usually she would read a few scriptures before going to bed, but tonight she went to her closet and took out an old photo album she kept on one of the shelves.

She carried it back to the bed and smiled as she opened it to the first page. Most of the pictures were from her life in high school and her eyes immediately fell on one of her and Mark. She wore her cheerleading uniform and he had his arms wrapped around her, both of them with wide smiles. They appeared so happy, and by all accounts, they were.

The hurt and anger did not come until later. She flipped through several pages and touched each picture, a feeling of nostalgia washing over her.

High school had been pretty good to her overall, and some[illegible] she missed those days.

One photo, however, made her smile turn into a scowl. There had been seven girls on the cheer squad that year, and one girl in particular Jenny still held a grudge against. She was not sure if she was still angry with Cindy or if her anger stemmed from the inability to let go of that grudge, but whatever it was, Jenny could not stop the knot of bitterness that raged inside her as she slammed the cover shut and dropped the album to the floor.

Why did the past suddenly have to rear its ugly head like this? She had so many good memories, but for some reason, Mark's leaving and the way she felt about this girl seemed to rise above the rest. Well, whatever the past was trying to tell her, she would not allow it to steal her sleep like it was sapping her happiness at this moment; she had to get up for work in the morning. However, she needed to find some way to find forgiveness, for both Mark and Cindy.

## *Chapter Five*

It was just past seven when Jenny pulled up to an empty parking space and got out of the truck. There was still a bit of sun left on the horizon, and she pulled her leather jacket out from behind the seat. Although it was still relatively early in the evening, the square was almost deserted.

Tourist season had ended abruptly, as it did every year, and the exhausted local people typically spent the first few weeks recovering by staying home and enjoying some peace and quiet. Even the park that sat in the middle of the square stood empty, and the street that wrapped around it had a scattering of cars, the majority parked in front of the Five Star Theater, their owners more than likely enjoying the latest flick on one of the two screens available there.

Jenny put on the jacket and pulled the collar close to keep the cool breeze from chilling her. Fall came early in the mountainous area, but that was fine with Jenny; the heat could be stifling in Colorado during the summer.

A Taste of Heaven, a local dining favorite, was located at the end of a long stretch of businesses in the Town Square on Elm Street. The owner was Kayla Brady, who had been the cheerleading coach at one time, though that had been ten years before Jenny attended.

Around ten people, mostly couples, were scattered around the diner when Jenny entered. The place had a classic diner look to it with a line of booths along the outer walls and two rows of tables down the center, all covered with the classic red and white checkered tablecloths. At a small table near the kitchen door sat one man Jenny had come to see. Mark.

Despite the many misgivings she had had the previous night, Jenny could not stop the smile that came of its own accord when he stood up, his navy-blue blazer complementing his dark hair quite well. He had always been a good dresser.

"Hey," Mark said as Jenny walked up, "I'm glad you came."

"You sound as if you thought I might not," she replied with a raise of a single eyebrow.

He shrugged but did not respond as they took a seat across from each other.

Jenny glanced around and saw Sam, Kayla's daughter, walking out of the kitchen. She gave the girl a wave and Sam held up a finger as if to say, 'just a minute', and walked over to a couple in the corner.

Mark sat silently across from her as he studied his menu as if he were cramming for a history final.

"You seem quiet," Jenny said. "Is everything all right?"

"Yeah, I'm fine," he replied without looking up. "I'm just hungry or something." He laughed as he set the menu down on the table and then picked up his fork and started playing with it.

Jenny could have cut the tension with a knife. "I'll tell you what," she said lightly, "let's order and then we can talk about Hollywood." She gave him the best smile she could, and it seemed to work as he visibly relaxed.

"Great idea," he replied.

One thing that struck Jenny since she first saw Mark two days earlier was how reserved he had become. After their initial meeting, he had become unusually quiet today hardly speaking two words to her at work. In the past, he had been loud and boisterous, and she could never get him to shut up. Now, however, it was as if he was the exact opposite, a fact she attributed to them not seeing each other for some time.

Sam came walking up, an order pad in her hand, and Jenny smiled at her. "Hey, Coach," she said as she leaned over and gave Jenny a hug. "How am I doing so far? Do you think I'm captain material?" She flashed a smile and Jenny laughed.

"Trying to butter me up, huh?"

Sam shrugged. "I can't lie to you," she replied with a mischievous grin. "Yes, I am." Then she took on a serious stance that showed she was ready to play her part as a waitress. "Okay, what can I get you both tonight?"

Mark did not even allow Jenny time to respond. "Two chicken sandwich plates, cheese fries, and two Cokes," he said before clapping the menu shut and handing it to Sam. Then he paused and looked at Jenny. "Is that right?"

Jenny nodded. It was still her favorite plate and apparently Mark had not forgotten, which somehow surprised her. Why would he remember something so trivial about her after being off doing exciting things in Hollywood?

Sam collected Jenny's menu. "You got it," she said. "I'll bring the drinks out in a minute." Then she walked away.

"I can't believe Kayla's daughter is in high school already," Mark said as Jenny watched the girl walk away. "Man, time sure does fly."

Sam returned and set their drinks and straws on the table and then left them alone again.

"Yeah, time does fly," Kayla replied as she took the wrapper off the straw and pushed the straw into the glass. "So, tell me about Hollywood. Why'd you decide to come back?"

Mark busied himself with his straw before responding. "I don't know where to begin," he replied after what Jenny thought was quite a bit of time. "There are a million unemployed actors out there, all of them waiting for their big break." He took a sip of his Coke before continuing. "You know about my Big Dave's Burgers commercial, right?"

Jenny nodded. "I do," she replied. "You did great in it."

He gave a tiny snort. "I thought that the exposure I got from that would have the casting calls rolling in," he said. "But they didn't. I did a few local commercials and there was a walk-on role on Criminal Masterminds, but that was about it." He shook his head sadly. "And my reason for coming home? I don't know. I guess you get to the point where you realize you're a failure and it's time to come back and admit defeat."

Jenny scrunched her brow; Mark never talked like that. "Hey," she said quietly, "you're not a failure. You went to pursue your dream and had some success. More than most people do in life."

She found it difficult to stay angry with him, especially when he was being so hard on himself.

He shrugged as he continued to stare at the table. "Maybe." Then he looked up at Jenny. "Anyway, what about you? What's new in the life of Jenny Hunter?"

She laughed. "I don't know where to begin," she replied.

However, before she could continue, Sam returned and set a plate of food in front of each of them, a smile on her face. "I applied my employee discount to the bill," she said as she set a slip of paper upside down on the table. "Enjoy." Then she was gone.

Jenny went to reach for the check, but Mark laid his hand on top of hers. A jolt of electricity moved through her, and she welcomed the sensation for a moment before looking up and gazing into his eyes.

All she could see was the hurt he had caused her, and she pushed away the warm feelings and locked them away into the back of her mind. She might be able to turn aside the animosity she felt for him, but she was unwilling to return to those old feelings she had had for him before.

"Let me pay," he insisted.

She pulled the check toward her. "No, I got it," she said firmly as she set the paper beside her plate. "As for what I've been up to. After graduation, I hung out here in Hopes Crest for the summer. My parents moved to Florida and left me the house, so I'm still there, which is nice."

Mark nodded and took a bite of his sandwich, a blob of ketchup dropping onto his blazer. A typical Mark move.

Jenny could not help herself; she laughed and handed him her napkin.

"Thanks," he said as he made a feeble attempt to wipe at the red stain.

As they ate, they talked, and for the next twenty minutes he gave her his utmost attention as Jenny shared things that had happened in Hopes Crest while Mark had been gone.

The conversation was not very deep, but she was glad to catch up with him. She was disappointed she really did not get much out of him about his time in California.

When they finished eating, they sat in an uncomfortable silence until Jenny took out a twenty-dollar bill and set it on the table on top of the check. "Well, it's been good catching up," she said as she stood up and collected her coat from the back of the chair. "I'll see you at work on Monday."

Mark stood up so quickly from his chair that it scraped loudly across the floor. "Jenny," he said as she turned around to leave, "I need to tell you some more stuff." He glanced around the nearly empty diner and added, "In private?"

Jenny's heart raced a little. There were things she wished to tell him, as well, but she was not sure her emotional state could handle it. Yet, she had put it all off long enough. Maybe this was what she needed to get her life going once again. "What do you have in mind?" she asked hesitantly.

"I'll grab some coffees from Penny's and meet you at the corner bench in the park. I doubt there's anyone there right now, so it'll be pretty private."

"Fine," Jenny replied. "I'll meet you there."

***

The wind was chillier than it had been earlier, but not nearly as cold as it would be in just a few months, as Jenny crossed Elm Street and made her way to the corner bench in the park. The playground sat empty, the swings swaying to and fro as the quickening air blew past them. Most of the businesses were closed, with only a few holding on to hope they would be able to glean a few more late sales before winter set in.

Mark arrived in no time with two cups of coffee and handed her one, steam rising through the small drink hole in the lid. "You know, I remember two kids coming out here on a Saturday night a long time ago," he said as he took a seat next to Jenny on the bench.

"Yes, I remember, all right," Jenny replied. "They were thirteen, had sneaked out of their houses and rode their bicycles here so they could..." Her words trailed off as she looked down at her coffee cup.

"Pledge their love to each other," Mark finished for her.

Jenny pushed the memory from her mind as she took a sip of her coffee. The weak light from a nearby lamppost lit up Mark's face, and she wondered why she had agreed to this.

Mark leaned back on the bench. "I wouldn't mind returning to that night and visiting that boy," he said as he stared off over the empty park. "I'd tell him what a lucky guy he was and that there was no other girl like Jenny in the world. And whatever you do, don't blow it."

Jenny could not stop the wave of emotions that rose in her. She shook her head. "Mark, I don't want to go down memory lane anymore tonight," she said. "Say what you need to say, please; I need to get going soon." In all honesty, she did not have somewhere else to be, but she was not ready for rehashing what they supposedly had. Not yet, anyway.

"The boy who dumped you on prom night was a fool," he said quietly. "He was self-centered, obnoxious, and thought he owned the world. What I said to you, the pressure I put on you to come back to my place—to move to California with me..." His voice trailed off and he let out a heavy sigh. "I'm so sorry, Jenny. I'm sorry I treated you like I did. There was no excuse for it, but I need to know something." He looked at her pleadingly but all she could do was sit and stare at him. "Can you forgive me?"

Jenny could not stop her eyes from widening in shock. She had never heard him once apologize to anyone for anything before. He sounded sincere, and his change in demeanor threw her off, but she could not shake off the feeling of betrayal that still clung to her heart.

"I don't know," she said skeptically. "There's more that you haven't told me, I can tell."

"What do you mean?" he asked in an astonished voice. "Like the reasoning behind it?"

Jenny stood up so quickly she would have spilled her coffee if the lid had not been firmly on top of it. She refused to play his games.

"Good night, Mark," she said and walked away.

"Jenny?" Mark called after her. "What is it? What did I not tell you? I can get on my knees and beg if you want me to, but I need to know what else I did."

She stopped and whirled around to face him. "You know what?" she demanded. "It's not just how you dumped me. Do you realize you crushed me? Not only did I lose my boyfriend when you left, but I also lost my best friend." She could not stop the sob that escaped her lips.

A moment later, he was beside her, pulling her into a tight embrace. She hated the fact that he had made her cry yet again, but she could do nothing to stop the tears from flowing or to pull herself from his arms.

"I am so sorry," he whispered in her ear. His voice sounded choked and she pulled away to look into his eyes. Though his words were sweet and his voice kind, the hurt he had caused all those years ago was too great.

"Mark," she said as she wiped at her cheeks, "I forgive you. I forgive you for crushing me that night, but I can't forget. I don't think I ever will."

He stared at her for a moment and then gave her a quick nod. "I needed that," he said finally. "God knows how long I've needed that. Thank you. Your forgiveness means everything. Have a good evening." Then he walked back to sit on the bench, and Jenny could only stare at him.

She was unsure what to make of the situation. On one hand, it felt good to forgive him. However, on the other hand, she had never seen him like this before. Mark Davis crying? It made no sense at all. Yet, she knew men did not enjoy an audience when they shed those rare tears, and she had said her peace, so she headed back to her truck.

Before opening the door, she turned back to look at him. Her brows scrunched together when he pulled something out of his inside coat pocket and brought it to his lips. Was that a flask?

Well, even if it was, it was none of her business. She had done the right thing by forgiving him, and now she could go back to trying to live a normal life.

Or at least something close to it.

## *Chapter Six*

The following Wednesday Jenny stood in the school gym, looking up at the lights above her. They were the same lights she stood under the night of her senior prom and danced the night away. She still had that blue prom dress at home in her closet, and though the night had been painful, it still was a memento she wanted to keep.

"Here they come," Molly said, breaking Jenny from her thoughts.

She turned and watched the boys walk into the gym in their shorts and t-shirts, ready for practice. Mark came in behind them, and even from this distance, she could see the dark circles under his eyes.

"Should I go ahead and send the girls home for the day?" Molly asked.

"Sure," Jenny replied. "Let me talk to them real quick." She walked over a few steps to where the girls were practicing a few basic moves. "All right, ladies, listen up." She waited for the girls to quiet down and make a half-circle around Molly and her, a few of them breathing hard from the exertion of their new routine. "As you know, school starts next week."

Moans and words of anguish and torment echoed around Jenny, and she let out a laugh. Oh, how she remembered doing much the same when she was in school.

"That means we'll be having practice right after school. So, that means from three-thirty until about five, Monday through Thursday, you will be here at the gym. Any questions?"

"I have one," Mary called out. "When will you pick the captain?" Hurried whispers and a few squeals came from the girls, and Jenny heard Molly let out a heavy sigh.

Jenny raised her hand for silence. She was beginning to wonder if her coach had to put up with this back when she was in school but then realized that the poor woman probably had been just as frustrated. "Coach Molly and I will be deciding over the next few weeks. So remember, it's on and off the court."

Nina, an eleventh-grader who wore her hair in two pigtails almost all the time, raised her hand. Jenny nodded at her and the girl stepped forward. "When is the first game? And is it at home?"

"Good question," Jenny said. She could not remember off the top of her head, so she waved at Mark, and he came jogging over, the smile on his face wide.

"What's up?"

"When's the first game, Coach?" Jenny asked. "The twenty-first? I can't remember."

"Yep, it sure is," he replied, his smile never waning. "In Silver Ridge at seven."

Jenny gave him a perfunctory smile and turned back to the girls. Mark returned to the boys without another word. "Okay, you heard him, ladies. We'll have a game in about a month. Starting next week, the intensity of practice is going to increase."

Emma tilted her head and gave Jenny a questioning look. "Is it true you and Coach Mark used to be together?" she asked.

Molly waved her hand in an attempt to shush her daughter, but Jenny only laughed. "Yes, we were, back in high school."

"Why'd you break up?" Brianna asked.

Molly blew her whistle, making Jenny jump. "Okay, enough. This is not history class or Gossipfest. We'll see you all on Monday; enjoy your time off because it's the last you're going to have for a while!"

The girls turned and headed toward the door and Jenny turned to Molly. "Thanks so much for that," she said. "One thing about small towns is everyone knows your business."

Molly looked as if she would fall over on the spot. "I'm so sorry about Emma. I'll have a talk with her later."

Jenny waved her off. "It's not a problem. At least it's out of the way now and we can move on."

Molly smiled. "That's true. Girls can be a catty bunch, can't they? Well, these girls need to learn that it's really none of their business." She untied the sleeves of the jacket she had tied around her waist. "Well, I'm going to head out now, unless you need me? I told Emma we could go grab something to eat."

"No problem. See you at church Sunday?"

"Definitely," Molly said and then shook her head as she stared off past Jenny.

Turning to look, Jenny followed her gaze and watched as one of the basketball players stood talking to Emma, a wide smile on his face.

"So it begins," Molly said, with a sigh. "The teenage years of falling in love. It's sweet, but it's going to be crazy dealing with her." She laughed and then headed over toward her daughter.

Jenny stifled a giggle as she watched Molly separate the two teens, glad she was not at the point of having to keep teenagers away from each other.

Then she turned around and watched as the boys ran their drills. Her eyes went to Mark as she thought about Molly's words of teenage years and love. It was a good thing Molly seemed ready to deal with all that because Jenny certainly could not have.

***

The squares in the planner that stared back at Jenny from her desk began to swim together, and she pressed her fingers on the bridge of her nose. Not only would she have her job as cheer coach, she would also be running girls' phys ed for the last two periods of the school day.

Granted, it was not that busy of a schedule, but she also had to coordinate her schedule with all of the sports so the cheer team could attend those games to show their school spirit, not just the basketball team.

At least she would have Molly as her assistant; her help would relieve some of the stress this year. Not that it had been all that bad before, but the extra help was going to come in handy.

Jenny found that dealing with a group of teenage girls could be almost overwhelming for one woman; but with two to share in the balancing of moods and possible emotional outbursts made it feel that much more manageable.

The office door opened and Mark walked in. "Sorry to bother you," he said quietly before making his way to the small desk in the corner. He looked hilarious with his large frame sitting in the low school chair and Jenny could not help but laugh. "What?" he asked over his shoulder.

"Okay, you look ridiculous sitting there," she said. "We're going to have to get you a bigger desk. I'll let janitorial know."

"I appreciate it," he said before turning back to his notebook where he began writing.

Jenny returned to her planner but kept glancing over at Mark, feeling bad about the way he sat hunched over the desk. She had not realized it was a desk better suited for an elementary school rather than a high school. With a sigh, she moved a stack of papers from the left side of her desk and said,

"Hey, why don't you come and share this desk with me. If you want."

"Thanks," he said with a smile as he grabbed his notebook before standing and turning the chair around. "My back and knees were about to blow out." Well, at least he did not have to sit hunched, even if the chair was still a bit low to the ground.

He returned to whatever he had been working on, his head down, and Jenny let out a sigh as she studied his dark hair. She always had a thing for his hair, the way it was so unruly and wild, much like he was.

Or rather used to be. He glanced up and she quickly looked away. No, that same person was still inside him, somewhere. He could pretend he was sorry for everything that had happened, but much more would have to take place for her to buy it as truth.

A short time later, he closed his notebook and set his pencil on top of it. "I'm heading out to grab a pizza," he said. "You're welcome to join me."

"No thanks," Jenny replied. She placed her elbows on the desk.

"Mark, listen, I want you to know something." She played with the pen in her hands before continuing. "I've been dating, and, well, I have a date tonight. I think we should really leave our relationship as professional."

He nodded. "I get it," he replied. Then he leaned back in the chair. "I'm curious. Are we at least friends?"

The question caught Jenny off-guard and she was not sure how to respond. Friendships with old flames led to nothing but disaster, or so she had heard. They had been friends first and a couple later, and that had ended in heartache. It was not as if she had a lot of experience with old flames. He had been the only one, but it was just too much of a risk, at least at this point.

"Like I said," she replied firmly, "we are professional colleagues. Nothing more." She pushed back her chair, picked up the planner and grabbed her purse. Mark stood as well. She hoped he would not try to talk her into going out with him because she feared she might give in all too easily, and she was not ready to take that step.

"Jenny," he said in a low voice, as if he had read her mind, something he had seemed to have been able to do when they were together, "just to let you know, I won't ask again." His voice had a hint of reluctance to it. "Anyways, I hope you have a great weekend."

She nodded, afraid to say anything in response, as she moved past him toward the door and found herself rushing down the hallway. She would stop by the janitorial office and have a desk delivered for him and then head home.

At least she had the weekend to herself before the school year started, and to allow her some time to wrap her head around the new Mark who shared an office with her.

***

Jenny forced a smile and then took another slice of pizza off the silver pan and set it on her plate. She was at By the Slice, the only pizzeria in town. Only a handful of people sat in the dining room, and across the table of the small booth sat her date, a man named Doug.

This was their second date, and like all of her others, she had nothing in common with the man. He loved documentaries while she liked comedies. He preferred nonfiction, and she adored romance. The list could go on forever, but she had accepted his invitation for another date despite their incompatibilities.

She found him to be a very nice man with a politeness about him, something so many men seemed to lack these days, or at least the ones she had dated lately.

Over the past few years, Jenny guessed she had gone on at least thirty dates, and very few of them went beyond the second. Plus, maybe there could be some sort of common ground between her and Doug where there had not been with the others.

"You know," Doug said between bites of his pizza, "I have to admit I was surprised that you accepted my offer for a second date."

"Oh?" Jenny said. "Why's that?"

"To be honest, you're very beautiful, and well, I don't have much in the looks department." His face reddened significantly, and Jenny's heart went out to him.

He was not what most women would consider overly handsome with his large glasses and crooked smile, but he was cute in his own way. He was also sweet and never lacked topics of conversation. The only real problem was that much of what he wished to discuss was of little interest to her.

"Aww, you're a handsome guy," she said with a smile. "Don't ever say you're not. And thank you for the compliment."

He leaned forward, a huge grin on his face. "Your eyes, they bring joy to one's heart," he said.

Jenny wanted to laugh, but she held it back. The poor guy was trying so hard, though she had to admit it was cute. "Thank you," she said.

"So, how was work this week?" he asked. She had shared on their first date about her job as coach, and she was honored that he remembered. "Are the girls learning fast enough?"

"They are," she replied. "Many of the girls were on the squad last year, and the new ones are catching up quick enough."

The front door to the restaurant opened, a cool breeze blowing through, and Jenny turned her head to see who had entered. Her eyes widened when Mark came walking through, a woman Jenny had not expected to see on his arm.

Cindy Peterson, a fellow former cheerleader who Jenny cared little for, still was really pretty with her blond hair and those 'attributes' boys in school often discussed in the locker room. Jenny watched as the two made their way to an empty table.

Though she had seen Cindy here and there around town, Jenny had not really talked to her in years. She wondered if Cindy was still the same person but then considered that maybe they had both grown up over time.

However, when Cindy removed her coat, Jenny realized Cindy had not changed at all. She wore jeans so tight they looked as if they had been painted on and an even tighter shirt, clearly still using her body as a means to wrap men around her finger.

"Uh, Jenny?" Doug asked, breaking her from her thoughts.

"Yes?" she said, pulling her eyes from the couple across the room and giving Doug a small smile. Mark could date whomever he wanted; it had nothing to do with her.

"Are you okay? You seem to be staring at that couple. Do you know them?"

"Who? Them?" Jenny asked, looking back over. Why was Mark's smile so big as he talked to Cindy? "Yeah, sort of."

She turned back to Doug. She reminded herself that it was none of her business, and she was being unfair to her date.

She grabbed another slice of pizza. "I'm really hungry," she said. "Now, I want to hear more about that computer program you're writing."

She didn't really want to hear about it, but it was something to keep him yapping. Try as she might, she could not stop herself from wondering whether Mark and Cindy were now a thing. If Doug was kept busy, it would give her time to see what the couple was up to. She just could not help herself.

Giving Doug a few nods here and there, Jenny kept glancing over and, for some reason, she felt a knot of anger form in the pit of her stomach.

Cindy was playing with her straw, her smile wide as the pair laughed together, and that knot tightened even more. Jenny knew Cindy had had a crush on Mark back in high school, and she had even gotten Cindy to admit it. Did the girl think she could try to steal him again?

"So, I figure I can finish it up in the next month," Doug was saying. "Then I'll present it to my boss. Then it's payday time." He rubbed his hands together in anticipation, gave her a huge grin and barked out a high-pitched laugh, causing Cindy and Mark to glance over at their table.

Jenny was determined that they were not going to be the only ones to have a good time tonight. She laughed, as well, and her hand slapped the table. "I love it!" she said loudly. "Payday. You're such a great man, Doug."

Her eyes shifted over to the other table, and her heart raced when she realized that Mark was approaching her table, Cindy walking right up next to him. Without thinking, Jenny reached out and grabbed Doug's hand.

"I love hearing your stories," she said, and Doug's cheeks went a bright red.

"Hey, Jenny," Mark said as he came up to the table. "You remember Cindy, of course."

Jenny flashed the woman a fake smile and then looked back at Mark. "I sure do," she replied. She felt a twinge of guilt at how insincere she was being, but somehow she could not help herself. "Mark, Cindy, I want you to both to meet Doug." She gave Doug's hand a squeeze and Cindy and Mark said hello to him.

Jenny narrowed her eyes a bit at Mark, but then realized what she was doing and relaxed her features once again. "So, what are you two doing?"

"I found out Mark was back in town," Cindy said, a small smile creeping over her lips as she grabbed Mark's hand.

"We just had a few drinks over at The Outlaws and decided to get some food." Then she gave a shrug. "And maybe a movie later."

For a moment Jenny considered throwing her drink on her. "That's nice," she replied in an overly sweet tone. "Well, Doug and I have to get going, don't we, honey?"

Doug shot her a confused look but nodded his head nonetheless. "Uh, yeah," he said, standing up and placing money on the table.

"It was good seeing you again, Jenny," Mark said, his brows scrunched.

Jenny stood and grabbed her purse. When Cindy put her arm around Mark's waist, she knew it was time to get out of there before she completely exploded.

"Looks like the food is ready," Cindy said as she made a point of pulling Mark back toward the table.

Not to be outdone, Jenny grabbed Doug's hand. "See you kids around," she said, dragging Doug out the door. When they were finally outside, Jenny let out a deep breath and then let go of Doug's hand. "Well, I'm glad to get out of there," she said.

Doug crossed his arms over his chest. "I take it that was an ex-boyfriend?"

"What do you mean?" Jenny asked, feigning innocence. "That guy?"

"It's OK," he sighed with a dejected shrug. "I've seen it before. You're trying to move past him but you still can't." He shook his head. "I always get caught up in the middle. It's just my luck."

Jenny felt bad as how she had treated him dawned on her. "Doug, I used to date him years ago and I don't have any feelings for him anymore."

However, she could not stop herself from taking another forlorn look through the restaurant window. Jealousy bore through her as she watched Cindy move to sit next to Mark in the same booth seat.

"I better go," Doug said despondently. "Good luck, Jenny."

Jenny turned back to Doug and then leaned in and kissed his cheek. "Thank you, Doug."

He smiled and then turned and headed down the street. Jenny turned back and looked at Mark's table one more time. How could she be so jealous? What they had been so long ago was now over, and now there sat Cindy where Jenny had once sat.

Yet, was it a longing for what they had shared as a couple, or was it the loss of their friendship that was bothering her? She missed their walks around Elm Street as much as sharing a booth, so it could be either as far as she knew.

Well, the reality was that they were not a couple any longer. Whatever it was she was feeling, it was not worth worrying about. She was no longer that girl on prom night, and never would be again.

***

That night Jenny lay in bed unable to sleep, the night's events replaying in her mind. It was not just the jealousy that she had displayed toward Mark, or the mean glares she gave Cindy. It was how she had treated Doug. The man was kind and would have had every right to scold her or show his frustration. But unlike her, he had taken the high road.

Reaching over for her phone, she typed out a long text letting Doug know how sorry she was for the way she acted on the date. More importantly, she asked for his forgiveness.

No more than two minutes later a reply came back.

'Jenny, thank you for your apology, and yes, I forgive you. Things like this can be complicated and it would be best if you took your time. If you want to go out again, just let me know. Best of luck.'

Letting out a sigh, she sent a thank you text assuring him that she would text him during the week, a promise she meant to keep. After setting the phone back down, she realized something else she had not done. Prayed. God had always been her refuge in times of trouble, but for some reason she had tried to take the burden of her pain herself and it was futile.

Closing her eyes, she whispered her prayer out loud.

"Lord, ever since Mark came back into my life, I have been confused. Old pain is still gnawing at me and jealousy and anger are guiding my steps. Please allow me to be your light so I can walk the path you need to me walk on. Amen." Feeling a bit better, she decided to pray again; this time adding both Doug and Mark into her prayers. And though she did not want to, she prayed for Cindy as well.

## *Chapter Seven*

Mark walked along the sidewalk next to Cindy. He had bumped into her earlier on Elm street and, just as Cindy had explained to Jenny, the two went to The Outlaws, the local bar, had a few drinks and then shared in a pizza.

Now he was walking her to her car, but his mind kept going back to seeing Jenny. He had wanted so badly to kick that buffoon she was with out of his chair and to sit with her instead. Cindy was all right, but he really had no interest in her; his heart and soul still belonged to Jenny, and there was no room for anyone else.

They came to a stop at Cindy's Jeep. "Are you sure you don't want to catch a movie?" Cindy asked with a pout as she pretended to fix his collar. "We could always go back to my place and watch one if you'd rather be alone." She traced her tongue over her lips provocatively, but her actions did nothing to stir his interest.

"To be honest, I'm pretty tired," he replied. The disappointment on her face was obvious. "Maybe some other time?" He almost kicked himself for saying it. He had no interest whatsoever in seeing her again, and what he needed to do was be completely honest with her. What was it about feeling the need to lie to save someone else's feelings all the time? He hated that it happened and did not know of any other way around it. Maybe it was his loneliness speaking for him.

"Okay," she replied with clear reluctance. "You have my number and I have yours." She opened the door to the Jeep and then stopped and turned around. "Oh, one more thing."

"What's that?" he asked.

She leaned forward and placed a small kiss on his lips. "I've been wanting to do that for years," she said quietly, a tiny smile playing at the corner of her mouth. "Talk to you soon."

She slid behind the steering wheel and allowed him to close the door for her. Soon, the Jeep was driving away, and Mark felt relief rush over him.

He reached into his coat pocket and took a quick drink from the flask. The liquid burned his throat, but it took away the focus of the hurt in his heart. At least for the time being, anyway, but it always came back once the alcohol wore off.

Yet, at least he could have some reprieve. After taking one more sip for good luck, he stuffed the flask back into his pocket and crossed the road to the small-town park to sit on the corner bench he had shared with Jenny so many times before.

She had looked so beautiful tonight, and it was obvious she was still jealous of Cindy. He chuckled as he recalled that same jealousy years ago whenever Cindy would bat her eyelashes at him or even give him a simple wave. The same anger he had seen in Jenny back then was still there tonight, and it left him with mixed feelings.

It was nice to know she still cared enough about him, but the fact she had been on a date with another man was a little disconcerting. He had somehow had it in his head she would be sitting in Hopes Crest pining away for him or something silly like that; though, in reality, he knew deep down it had all been a part of his overactive imagination.

The man she had been with tonight was clearly head over heels infatuated with Jenny, but Mark also knew when she had no interest in something, and she certainly was not interested in that guy.

What he had hoped for was that, once he had returned to Hopes Crest, everything would simply fall back into place, more so when it came to Jenny. However, it had gone worse than he had expected.

She did not even wish to be friends with him, and honestly, who could blame her? What he had done was sickening. At least she had been willing to forgive him.

However, what he needed so badly right now in his life was the friendship they had once shared. The gentle words of encouragement she had for him, or even her willingness to pray for him. How he wished he would have told her how much she had inspired him when they were together.

"Mark?" a voice asked from behind him. "Mark Davis?"

He quickly returned the flask he had not even realized he had taken out of his coat again and turned around to see Pastor Dave, the man who was his pastor when he had been interested in going to church. A feeling of regret washed over him, but he pushed it aside. He did not have to answer to this man, or anyone, for that matter.

"Hey, Pastor," Mark said as he stuck out his hand.

Rather than shaking his hand, however, Dave pulled him in for a quick hug. "It's so good to see you," he said as he pulled away. "How long have you been back in town?" Dave looked the same as Mark remembered him. Short blond hair and always wearing a smile.

"Just a few weeks," Mark replied. "I've just been trying to get settled back in. How about you? Is church going well?"

"It is," Pastor Dave replied. "We're getting new members all the time." He took a seat on the bench and waited for Mark to sit next to him. "Speaking of, any chance you could pay us a visit sometime?"

Mark shifted a little. "Well, Pastor…" he started to say, but the Pastor cut him off.

"Hey, now, call me Dave. You're not a kid anymore."

Mark laughed. "Okay, Dave," he replied. It felt good that someone treated him as if he were now an adult, which made him feel as if he had made some changes, hopefully for the better. "You see, I don't really pray that much anymore, and I…well…"

He could not put into words what had happened to his spiritual life, and he felt kind of bad. Dave was a great guy, and Mark did not want to bash the church, but the last thing he wanted right now was religion.

"Mind if I tell you a quick story?" Dave asked as he turned and rested his arm on the back of the bench. "It won't take long and it shouldn't be too boring."

This made Mark laugh again. "Sure, go ahead," he replied.

"A long time ago, there was a man working as a bartender, and the weight of the world sat on his shoulders. You see, he had run off and married his girlfriend. They were living it up, or at least that's what they would tell themselves." He shook his head in wonderment. "But the reality of it was that things weren't as great as they pretended them to be. It got so bad that sometimes the pressure of everything would get to this man and soon he found himself sneaking shots of liquor in an attempt to numb the pain. But then every morning, do you know what he woke up with?"

"A hangover?" Mark asked. It made the most sense to him; how many mornings had he woken up with the hair of the dog?

Dave slapped his hand on his knee and barked a loud laugh. "You bet he did," he replied, "but that's not the point I was making. He also woke up with the same problems he had before he had numbed his brain." He took a deep breath. "Look, Mark, I'm not telling you what to do, and I don't want to come across as judgmental, but I used to carry a flask just like the one there in your pocket. There are other ways to deal with your pain, whatever that pain might be."

A heaviness weighed on Mark's heart. So much was going on with his life right now and he really needed someone to talk to. Jenny was clearly out of the question after what he had put her through, but maybe Dave would be willing to give him some of his time.

"Do you do, like, counseling or anything?" Mark asked carefully. "I really need someone to talk to."

Dave gave him a knowing smile as he stood up from the bench. "I do," he replied. "I'm always at the church on weekdays until around five or six. You stop in whenever you want and we'll have a chat."

Mark extended his hand. Just listening to the man's story had been uplifting. Maybe he had put blame in the wrong place. "Thanks, Pastor…I mean, Dave. And hey, I might just show up on Sunday."

"Good," Dave said as he gave Mark's hand a firm shake. "We'd love to see you again. Take care and I'll be watching for you."

Mark watched Dave walk away. Perhaps this was exactly what he needed, a chance to talk to another man about what was going on in his life.

He automatically reached for the flask in his pocket but then stopped. Though it took everything in him to remove his hand from the container, he did. If he was going to make any changes, he had to start at this very moment.

***

Sunday morning rolled around all too soon, a feeble sun in the sky doing little to warm the air. Mark gave himself a once-over in the mirror, adjusted his tie for the fiftieth time and then slipped on his navy-blue sports coat. He smiled. The suit fit him well, and even though he had not lifted weights in a few years, he was still in pretty good shape. Granted, no one would be able to appreciate his well-defined biceps in the jacket, but at least he knew he had not lost his athletic form just yet.

After one last glance to see if his coat fell correctly in the back, he reached into the drawer of his nightstand and pulled out a black leather Bible, his name embossed in gold on the lower right corner of the front cover. It had been a while since he had even opened the Book, but he did so now to read the inscription on the inside.

'Mark, He is the Light of the world. Let that Light always guide you. Love, Jenny.'

He read it one more time before closing the Book and heading out of the room. In the hallway, however, he paused. His parents were arguing in their bedroom again and he felt like a younger version of himself as he listened to his father shouting at his mother, as if everything that did not go his way had been her doing.

"It's not my fault you spoiled him!" Of course, they were discussing Mark again, and that only complicated his emotions. "He threw away a chance at the pros with this foolish notion of becoming some sort of movie star."

"Harold," his mother replied in a soothing tone, "he went to follow a dream. We've always encouraged him to do that. Stop being so angry at him."

Mark cringed after she said those words. He knew what would follow.

"Shut your mouth!" his father shouted. Just as Mark expected. "Don't you dare tell me what to do!"

Mark bit his lip to keep from shouting. His parents had fought for years, and he knew his dad was disappointed in him for not pursuing his baseball career. No, it was much more than disappointment; he resented Mark for it, and he never allowed a moment to pass without reminding him of that fact.

The arguing continued as Mark walked down the hallway and out to his truck. As he pulled the truck out of the driveway, it took every ounce of energy in him to keep his anger in check.

It had been his father who wanted him to play baseball since Mark began walking. It was Mark's father who made him stay hours after practice perfecting his swing. Going pro had always been his dad's dream, but it was the one single thing in Mark's life Mark did not want to do.

His thoughts went to his mother, and he felt bad for her. She had always been so supportive of what he wished to do with his life and his father's rants and raves never deterred her from that fact.

Many a night she had sat with Mark while his father screamed at the television or stormed around his office after having consumed too many beers, waiting for that moment when the man's temper would finally explode.

Then began the second phase of his rampage against house and home as he threw anything he could get his hands on against the walls with a loud curse. Through it all, his mother protected Mark from his father's wrath.

The parking lot of the church loomed before Mark and he stared wide-eyed, unable to believe how long he had been lost in thought. He did not even remember passing the intersection with the town's only stoplight or making the half-lap drive around the park in the middle of the Town Square. When he slid the truck into a parking space, he shook his head to clear out the cobwebs of old memories.

What good would those memories do him now? Not a bit of good at all.

The relative silence that followed after he turned off the engine relieved the pulsing in his head only slightly, and he reached over to grab a flask from the glove box.

He took a long drink and then screwed the lid back on, wondering if he should take the flask with him. He chuckled as he realized that was probably not the best idea he had ever had, and he threw the flask back into the glove box. No, he probably should not take it with him. Not to church.

With Bible in hand, he headed toward the entrance, weaving between the cars to where people stood at the entrance waiting to file inside. Small groups of members chatted with each other while children chased one another across the grass, and Mark smiled at the people he had known since he was a kid. They all greeted him as if he had never been gone, and a feeling of calm fell upon him at the familiarity of it all.

It did not take long for the line to dwindle and for him to get through the double doors that led to the foyer where more people greeted him with a quick handshake or a wave. He returned with the same but did not stop to talk long.

Instead, he entered into the nave, where he stopped to look up at the large wooden cross that stood against the wall behind the pulpit. That cross had once held a deep meaning for him, and the memories came crashing in on him of an eleven-year-old boy walking up to stand before that cross and the congregation as he asked the Lord into his heart. Was that nearly twelve years ago?

"Mark, you decided to show up!" Dave said, breaking Mark from his thoughts. "Hey, I love the sports coat; it looks great."

Mark looked down at his jacket and smiled. "Thanks," he said, taking the hand Dave offered him and giving it a firm shake. "I'm glad I came today. I'm looking forward to it."

The choir began to sing and Dave glanced at his watch. "It looks like we're starting a minute early," he mused. "I'm going to have Dolores take care of you. You remember her, don't you? She helps new and returning members get back into the swing of things, so to speak."

Mark went to respond, but Dave was already hurrying away. He knew Dolores Van Schneider as the old woman who was always complaining about something, whether it be at church or the local PTA meetings his mom used to attend when Mark was still in school. He knew she meant well when it came to her responsibilities for the town, but the last thing he wanted was to be forced to sit next to her for the next hour.

However, there was no mistaking that it would be the case when he saw Dave talking to the gray-haired woman and pointing at Mark. As mean as it was to think, Mark could not help but be reminded of one of the Wicked Witches from Oz in her black dress and silver-framed glasses that hung from a chain around her neck.

"Hello, Markus," Dolores said as she scuttled up to him. "I didn't know you were back in town. You do remember me, don't you?"

The arrogance on her face was so evident, as if she thought everyone should know who she was. And of course, they did, but not for the reasons she probably thought.

She was the kind of person who needed to be a part of everything, and in charge of it all, too. No one else was as good as she was, nor could they do any job as well as she could. She had gone so far as to say as much at a meeting Mark overheard when he was in high school. Even as a young adult, he found her to be self-possessed. How no one ever pointed this out to the woman, he never knew.

Perhaps someone had at one point in her life but she ignored the advice; he would not put it past her.

"I do," he replied. "And it's Mark."

She gave a derisive sniff. "I believe Markus is much more fitting a name, but alas, you are an adult now. Well, come sit with me. I always sit in the front row where I can be closer to the Pastor." Her voice dripped with pride.

Mark's heart sank, but he figured she would at least be quiet while the pastor gave his sermon.

Before he could take a step to follow her, however, someone called out to him. "There you are! I've been looking all over for you."

Mark turned and his heart soared. Jenny stood beside him, a smile on her face. Wearing a deep blue sleeveless dress, she looked like royalty. Her dark hair was pulled back into a French braid and she wore just enough makeup to be alluring, at least to him. For a moment, he wondered if he was going to pass out, but whether it was from the relief that rushed over him or how close she now stood to him, he was not sure.

"Thank you, Dolores," Jenny said as she slid her arm into the crook of his elbow, "I'll take it from here."

Dolores gave another disapproving sniff. "Well, I never," the older woman snapped. Then she pointed a manicured finger at Jenny. "If, in the future, you wish to be a part of the welcoming committee, I would suggest you attend our meetings." And with that, she turned and stormed off to take her seat in the front row.

Mark turned to Jenny. "Hey, thanks for that. I was worried about having to sit with her. I remember all too well how annoying she can be."

Jenny laughed. "It's no big deal," she replied. She removed her arm from Mark's and he immediately felt as if a part of him was missing. "I wouldn't want anyone to sit with her."

Mark smiled and then looked around at the packed pews. "So, any idea where I should sit?"

She bit her lip before she replied. "Well, you can sit with me and Katie if you'd like…for today." He gave her a nod and then she looked down at his hand. "Is that the same Bible I gave you?" she asked.

He lifted it to show his name stamped on the front. "It sure is," he replied. "I could never get rid of it."

She gave him a thoughtful look and then nodded before heading down the aisle. He followed behind her and took the seat next to her at the end.

As the choir continued with their song, Mark glanced around. There were so many faces he recognized. There was Kayla from the diner sitting next to her best friend Susan. Parents of the kids he used to play baseball with. Julie from the video shop. So many memories.

He sneaked a glance at the woman at his side, and despite the fact he was now among so many people he had known all his life, that feeling of loneliness and longing returned.

## *Chapter Eight*

Jenny groaned as another basketball came bouncing past her at lightning speed and hit Emma square in the arm, causing the poor girl to yell out in pain and anger. She grabbed the ball from Emma and turned just as Mark walked up.

What was it about this man and his not wanting to wait to start practice until the cheer team had completed theirs? She would not have minded sharing the space if the boys could keep control of the basketballs a little better, but they flew around the room willy-nilly, and her squad could only take so many hits.

"Hey, sorry about that, Coach," Mark said as he came walking up.

She pulled back the grimace that threatened to cross her face and handed him the ball. She was being overly obstinate and there was no reason to be. Mark had been nothing but polite and it was not as if she owned the gym herself or something.

Mark threw the ball back to a pair of boys waiting under a nearby hoop. "Are you guys almost done for the evening?"

Jenny nodded. "We are in just a few minutes," she replied. Then she glanced over at the boys behind him. "How's your team looking?"

"You know, not bad, really. I think we might be able to go far this season." His smile was wide as he gave her a wink. "Of course, the boys are much more motivated when the girls cheer them on." He laughed and Jenny joined him.

"Don't I know it," she said. "It's how couples meet." She bit her lip. Why did she have to say that? "Anyway, I need to get back to the girls. I'll talk to you later."

He nodded and she turned back around and stopped as the girls all stood staring at her. Molly had three girls to the side working on jumps, but the rest stood side by side whispering and giggling to each other.

"Okay, ladies, what's so funny?"

"We just think it's cute how you and Coach Mark used to date," Amanda said. "And now you're both coaches. Sounds romantic to me." The girls burst out laughing.

Jenny felt her cheeks heat up but couldn't help but laugh herself, mostly because of the way they were so amused. She remembered not too long ago acting very much the same as them when it came to who was dating whom.

"Well, that was a long time ago. We're professional colleagues now and nothing more." The girls snickered, but Jenny ignored them. "I wanted to let you know that I'm proud of the way you've been working hard. Each and every one of you has done a great job."

Molly walked up with her trio, who joined the others in the line.

"So, this Friday, we're going to do something a bit different." She nodded at Molly, who jogged over to the bleachers and came back with a stack of papers in her hand.

"This is a permission slip to go and get some food on Friday night at By the Slice. After we eat, we'll go to Retrocade for some fun. Since this will be an official school function, you'll need a parent's signature and they'll need to pick you up at the arcade no later than ten. Any questions?"

The girls were talking a mile a minute and Molly leaned in and whispered, "I think I know what's coming next."

"Me too," Jenny said as Mary raised her hand. Jenny nodded at her, and Mary smiled.

"Will any boys be going?" A chorus of high-pitched giggles echoed around the gym.

Jenny nodded her head, though it had a bit of reluctance to it. "Yes, the boys will be going, as well. We'll be traveling and interacting as a team. This is not a hook-up night."

This brought on another bout of giggles, some of the girls going so far as to double over in laughter. Jenny gave them a pointed look. "There'll be chaperons, but take the opportunity to bond with each other; you're going to be working side by side for the next few months and some of the best friendships come from being on a squad." The girls nodded, the laughter having died down. Jenny turned to Molly. "Did I forget anything?"

"Girls, we'll be leaving in cars from the school. We want to be perfectly clear, you'll not be leaving with any boys. I don't care if you're going out with them or not, this isn't date night. Also, if your parents want to come, they may."

Jenny held back a giggle when she heard "No way" and "I hope not!". She had said pretty much the same things when she was still in high school and the suggestion was made to her and her teammates. A moment later, the group was dismissed.

"Well, what do you think?" Jenny asked Molly. "Do you think it'll go over fine?"

Molly smiled. "They're good kids," she replied firmly. "What could possibly go wrong?"

***

"What could possibly go wrong?" Jenny mumbled as she headed through the arcade toward Katrina, who stood wiping tears off her cheeks as they rolled down her face. It was just after eight and the pizza party next door had gone well. The boys and girls sat around in their groups, the girls laughing as the boys showed off for them.

Once they got to the arcade, however, everything had soured significantly.

"Katrina, what's wrong, sweetie?" Jenny asked as she walked up to the dark-haired ninth-grader.

Katrina looked up, her heavy mascara running down her cheeks. "It's Brandon and Mary." She glanced over to a far corner and jutted out her chin as a way to point them out. "Take a look."

Jenny turned her head and followed Katrina's gaze. The two teens Katrina had mentioned stood next to each other playing a video game together. "I don't see the problem," she said slowly, still trying to figure out what was going on.

"He didn't ask me to play," Katrina whined. "Why is he playing with her? She's trying to steal him." She shook her head. "If she touches him, I'm going to give it to her, Coach. I'm sorry, but I won't allow my man to be stolen."

Jenny bit at her lip to keep from smiling and put her hand on Katrina's shoulder. Oh, the joys of being a teen girl, how well she could remember. "I bet that Brandon only has eyes for you. I don't think he's interested in Mary."

Katrina raised her eyebrows. "Do you think so?"

"I know so," Jenny replied. "Watch." She called out Brandon's name and he immediately turned and then hurried over.

"Hey, what's going on, Coach Jenny?" he asked and then looked over to Katrina. "Whoa, are you okay?" His voice was worried.

"Katrina's just having a bad day," Jenny explained. "We didn't want to disturb you while you were playing your game, isn't that right?" She gave Katrina a wink.

"Yeah, that's right," Katrina replied with a nod. "If you want to go back and play with Mary, I understand."

Brandon laughed and shook his head. "No, that's okay. She just came up and started playing next to me. I was actually hoping you'd join me, but I didn't know where you were."

He gave her a wide grin, and before Jenny could say another word, the two walked off and found another game to play together.

Letting out a sigh, Jenny looked around the arcade. That was one disaster avoided. The rest of the teens seemed to be enjoying themselves.

Several parents had shown up, but not as many as Jenny had expected, which was fine by her; she did not need to get into yet another conversation about who would be captain and would their daughter be standing in the front or the back of the squad during games?

Jenny noticed the owner of A Taste of Heaven diner sitting at one of the tables and headed over to her. Kayla was still a very pretty woman with her red hair and green eyes, a fact that was evident by the two boys who stood with goofy grins on their faces as they stared over at her from one of the video games.

Kayla looked up when Jenny approached her. "How're you holding up?" she asked.

"Oh, you know," Jenny replied. "Dealing with one teenager is bad enough. Now times that by twenty. I had to prove to Katrina that Brandon wasn't dumping her, and earlier I had to stop two from trying to make out in the corner." She shook her head. "I don't remember doing that in high school, do you?"

"No way," Kayla said with a laugh. "My parents would've tanned my hide if I tried anything like that! But I knew a few who did. I sure hope that what I've taught Sam will keep her from making those kinds of choices, but all I can do is keep teaching and otherwise hand it over to God."

Mark walked by and Jenny could not stop the smile that came to her face. He ambled over to one of the boys and the two were soon talking amicably together. Mark never struggled to make friends, and somehow Jenny was not surprised he still had the gift of gab.

"Listen, don't stress. You're doing fine," Kayla said. Jenny was glad the woman had not noticed her appraisal of Mark. "Sam won't stop talking about you." She gave Jenny and extra-wide grin. "Of course, I told her to listen to you at practice; you're by far a better leader than I ever was."

Jenny laughed and placed a hand on her hip. "Why, Kayla, are you trying to butter me up like your daughter has done over the last few weeks?"

Kayla shrugged. "I guess maybe a little," she replied with an exaggerated sigh. "But tell me, is she at least in the top three?"

Jenny raised an eyebrow. "Oh, you may never know," she said, knowing Kayla did not mean anything by her words. She was not as pushy as other parents, and Jenny found her to be a lot easier going. "The announcement will be made in just under an hour, so you're just going to have to wait like everyone else."

"Fine then," Kayla said in mock frustration.

Sam came rushing up, Emma at her side. "Hey, Coach, two boys are arguing over Emma." Emma's face flushed significantly, but Sam was all about sticking up for her best friend. "They can't decide who gets to play her in pool next and they're talking about actually fighting over it." She crossed her arms. "Boys are so dumb."

Jenny groaned. More drama. What had she been thinking taking on high school girls?

"I got this," Kayla said and she followed the girls to the back.

An elderly woman Jenny recognized as Bonnie Page, Denise's grandmother, walked up to Jenny. She was a short woman, a bit on the heavy side, and she walked with a limp. However, the woman was never seen without a wide smile on her face.

"Hello, Jenny," the woman said. "I just wanted to thank you for what you did for Denise."

Jenny waved a hand at her. "Oh, it was nothing. She's been a great help in the gym, so it worked out for the both of us."

"Well, that poor girl has been through more than her fair share of problems, so you just need to know that what you did for her has built up her confidence tenfold. I just wanted you to know that."

The woman's words sent a warm feeling through Jenny. "I'm glad to hear that. You've done a marvelous job with her; she's definitely a young lady with integrity."

Mrs. Page gave her an appreciative smile. "It's all her, I have to admit," she said. "Anyway, I just wanted to thank you and also let you know that I'm going to take her home when this is over."

"Thank you for letting me know," Jenny said with a smile. "And you have a great night."

Jenny sighed heavily and checked her phone. If she could make it another hour and a half, she was going to treat herself to a glass of wine when she got home.

She returned her phone to her pocket and moved to make another round of the arcade just as Louise and Evan Montgomery walked up.

Mary's parents tended toward the more stereotypical wealthy class with their superiority complex and their condescending glares and they made it known that they could buy whatever—and sometimes whomever—they wanted.

"Hello, Coach Jenny," Mrs. Montgomery said, her nose a little higher in the air than most.

"Mrs. Montgomery," Jenny replied.

The woman laughed. "Oh, now, please call me Louise," the woman said. "Missus makes me sound so old."

Jenny forced a smile, hoping they did not want to talk long. In all honesty, she found both of them to be a bit more high and mighty for her liking, but they were also the best monetary contributors to the team. Jenny did not like the idea of brown-nosing, but she could at least be cordial.

Then she was reminded of the prayer she had said about being a light for Christ. It was not meant only for those one liked; it was meant for everyone.

"Thank you again for your donation this year," Jenny said, knowing they would appreciate more recognition for what they had done, and in all honesty, it had been a generous gesture, even if they had ulterior motives in offering the contribution. "I know the girls love the new uniforms." She motioned Katrina over. "Katrina, what do you think of the new cheerleading outfits this year?"

Katrina smiled as she looked down at the blue and white skirt. "They're great," she replied. "Much better than last year's; we can actually breathe in these." Then she returned to where Brandon was playing some karate video game.

"That's lovely," Louise replied. "We've been considering purchasing a small bus exclusively for the cheerleading team."

"Oh, is that so?" Jenny asked her curiosity piqued.

"It is a very nice bus," Louise continued. Then a sly smile formed on her lips. "However, we're a bit worried about Mary." Jenny knew what was coming and did not look forward to hearing it, but she was not able to forestall the woman. "Our Mary is worried she won't make captain again this year," she continued. "That, of course, is nonsense. I told her that as soon as she wins, we're going to celebrate by buying the team that new bus. Is that not true, Evan?"

"You're right, dear," Mr. Montgomery murmured.

It suddenly occurred to Jenny that she had never really heard Mr. Montgomery speak, but looking him up and down, she garnered a guess. He was tall, very slim, and always walked with his shoulders drooped, looking more like a lowly butler whereas his wife dressed more like a queen.

It was no secret that the woman had extensive cosmetic surgery, especially since she bragged all around town about it. Whether it was her face or her breasts, nothing to the woman was sacred.

"Well, we really could use a bus," Jenny assured the woman. It was the truth, but she hated that no matter how she put it, her words would sound like she was only being nice to earn that new bus. "The team bus we have now is on its last legs."

Mark came walking up and Louise gasped. "Mark Davis," she said, bringing her hand up to smooth down her perfectly styled hair and batting her eyelashes as she looked him up and down. "Oh my, you have certainly grown." She placed a hand on his arm and squeezed his bicep.

Jenny could not believe her eyes. Louise was a married woman and she was openly flirting with another man right in front of her own husband.

"Louise," Mark said smoothly, "I must say, you look as stunning as ever. And, Evan, it's great to see you, as well. How's Brian?"

Louise did not allow her husband to reply. "Brian is well," she said. "He's attending medical school in New York and our Mary is on the cheer squad, hopefully soon to be captain again." Jenny did not miss the pointed look the woman shot at her.

"Really?" Mark replied with surprise. "I'm shocked you would allow that."

Louise's eyes widened. "Whatever do you mean?"

"Well, it's far more important to worry about positions when a student is a junior or a senior. The freshman and sophomore years are usually the time to work on academics so students can get into AP classes later. Then once they're in those higher-level classes, they can include team captains in whatever sport they are participating in.

When I was being scouted, that was what they considered for me. But if she wants the extra responsibility of being squad captain in lieu of better grades…" He shrugged. "Well, you know best."

Louise stared at Mark with consideration for several moments before turning to Jenny. "I do not wish you to believe we were only offering you the bus to simply obtain the position of captain for our Mary," she said meaningfully. "We'll have the bus delivered next week. And please, if you were planning on choosing Mary, I would ask that you do not, as a favor to me. She does not need the extra burden."

"Of course," Jenny replied. "And thank you. Thank you both for your generosity."

The couple began to move away, but Louise turned to Mark as she went to walk past him. "Thank you for your insight," she said. "And it is good to see you again." She gave Mark a hug, and Jenny's eyes widened when the woman gave Mark's rear a firm pat. Then a moment later, she smiled and they were quickly lost in the crowd.

"Wow, thanks, I guess," Jenny said to Mark as she stared at the place where she had lost sight of them. Then she giggled. "I didn't realize she was going to grab your butt."

Mark shrugged. "Whatever. It's cool. I'm glad you got the bus, though. I overheard them trying to bribe you, so I just wanted to help out."

Jenny smiled. Not only had he gotten her out of an awkward situation with a parent who had no misgivings of unleashing her wrath on anyone who went against her wishes, but they had gotten a new bus out of it, one she could share with the basketball team, or whichever team they would be traveling with.

Plus, she had not had to stoop to taking a bribe to get it. Not that she would have, of course; she would have kept the old bus and denied Mary the captain position simply because of the bribe. However, everything worked out in the end, since Mary was not who she and Molly had chosen as captain anyway.

She felt such great relief, an idea came to mind. "Hey, I'm going to have a glass of wine back at my place after all this is over. Would you like to stop by?"

Mark broke out into a huge smile, one she had not seen on him since before he left for California. "Sure," he replied. I'd like that. I'll see you then."

For the first time in a long time, Jenny thought about the possibility that she and Mark might actually become friends again, and the thought made her happier than she realized it would.

## *Chapter Nine*

Jenny pulled up in the driveway in front of her house and got out of the car, her hands wringing together nervously. When the headlights of Mark's car swung in beside her, she began to wonder if maybe inviting him over had not been such a good idea after all. She did not want to give him the wrong impression, but at the same time, she wanted the chance to talk to him.

"Hey, I remember that roof and window," Mark said, pointing to a window above the garage.

Jenny laughed as she looked up at her old bedroom, and her nervousness dissipated as quickly as a fog on a sunny summer morning. "I do, too," she replied. "How many times did you climb up there and sit outside while we whispered the night away?"

When she turned to look at him, he was already smiling at her. "Too many to count," he replied. "Wow, it looks taller now than it did then for some reason. It's crazy what love makes you do." He laughed and then grimaced. "Sorry. Anyway, thanks for inviting me over."

"Don't worry about it," she replied with a smile. She led him to the front door, which was unlocked, and into the living room where Katie was sitting on the couch. The woman was always changing her hair color, and today it was a deep brown with bands of red mixed in.

"Hey there, Slugger," Katie said as she walked over and gave Mark a hug. "How've you been? Sorry I didn't talk to you at church Sunday; I was caught up talking with Susan as soon as the service ended."

Mark laughed. "It's not a big deal," he replied. "And I'm doing great, thanks. I see you still dye your hair."

She brushed back a strand behind her ear. "Yeah, you know me," she said with a sideways grin. "I have always been a rebel." She gave a hearty laugh and then yawned. "Anyway, I need to hit the sack. Work tomorrow; the videos won't sell themselves. We'll have to catch up some other time." She gave Jenny a hug. "Have fun," she whispered in Jenny's ear so that Mark could not hear and then she was gone.

"So," Jenny said nervously, "does the house look the same?"

Mark glanced around the living room. "It does, for the most part," he replied. "I can't believe your parents left the house to you. That was really nice of them."

Jenny headed to the kitchen, which was only separated from the living room by a large island and counter. "It was," she said as she took out a bottle of wine and two stemmed glasses. "They wanted to move to Florida and didn't want to sell the house, so it made sense." She poured the wine and came back out to the living room and handed one to Mark. "And I didn't want to leave, so it worked out great for me."

"Why'd you decide to stay?" Mark asked as he took a seat on the other side of Jenny.

She wanted to tell him that it was because she hoped that maybe one day he would come back to Hopes Crest. That maybe, one day, just like in a fairy tale, all would be fine and things would be the way they once were. But now that four years had passed, she was not sure that was what she still wanted. So, instead, she replied, "Oh, you know, I'm a Hopes' girl. Born here and will live her for the rest of my life." She lifted her glass in the air. "Here's to you saving me earlier," she toasted.

He clinked his glass to hers and then took a drink. It was silent for a moment before Mark spoke up again. "You know, I'm not much of a wine drinker, but this is good," he said. "What is it? A fruit blast?"

Jenny laughed, almost spilling her wine, which would have been a disaster on the white cushions. Why her mother had insisted on white furniture, Jenny never knew, but somehow the woman had kept them spotless for years. "No," she replied to his question. "It's Moscato."

Then an image flashed before her, reminding her of something she had been wanting to ask him. "Do you carry a flask with you?"

He nodded reluctantly as he set his glass down on the coffee table. "I do," he replied. "It kind of helps take the edge off things. You know, when pressure builds a lot."

Jenny searched his face as she waited for the punchline. However, it never came. "But you're Mark Davis," she said when she realized he was being completely honest. "The Hero of Hope. When did things start getting to you enough to need to 'take the edge off'?"

He looked down at the cushion that separated them. "I've asked myself that same question quite often," he replied. "But I think it really started falling apart my senior year."

Jenny shook her head. There was no way she was going to be blamed for his problems.

She must have allowed her thoughts to show on her face because he paused and added with a great amount of emphasis, "No, it wasn't you, Jenny," he said. "It was me all along. And what people expected from me."

Jenny turned toward him. "I don't understand," she said quietly. "You could walk anywhere in town and people praised you. Every girl wanted you…like Cindy." The words hung in the air for several moments before Mark responded, and Jenny thought her heart would strangle her as she waited.

"Cindy," he said with a sigh. "Yeah, well, trust me, there's nothing going on there. It seems that, besides a few people, the old crew has moved on. But more to the point, everyone worshiped me in some far out, unrealistic way. In their eyes, I could do no wrong, and it began to weigh on me."

The idea that what other people thought of Mark bothered him was not something she had ever expected to hear. "Like how?"

Mark gave a light snort. "Where do I start?" he asked. "Teachers would up my grades, even if I hadn't done the work correctly, or even at all. I was told I was a role model for the younger kids, so I couldn't let them down, now could I? You see, everyone wanted to be a part of the Davis Express." His voice sounded cynical.

"I was going places, going pro, but no one stopped to ask me if that's what I wanted for my life."

Jenny's eyes widened. "You mean you didn't want the baseball career?" she asked in a shocked tone. It was all he talked about whenever they were together. Even the acting idea was a surprise when he had decided to leave for California. "I don't get it; you're so good at it."

"My dad wanted it," Mark said in an angry voice. "My earliest memories are of him teaching me how to play. At first, I loved it because it gave us something to do together. But as I got older, he pushed me harder. Me leaving for Hollywood was my chance to escape, to follow a dream that was all my own. I wanted to try something completely different and show my dad that I could make something of myself besides what he wanted for me."

He lifted the glass to his lips and downed the rest of his wine in one gulp. Then he set the empty glass back on the table.

He stared at the empty glass for several moments before looking up at her once again. "But there was one thing in my life I had always wanted, one thing that was solid, and that was you, Jenny," he said sadly. "I know I screwed up badly, and I know that me and you together as a couple isn't going to happen. But I need to be honest." His eyes clouded over and Jenny could see him fighting back tears. "I need a friend—a real friend. Not Cindy or Dale or any of the guys who wanted to be around me for the attention they could get for just being there. Someone who genuinely cares for me."

Jenny wiped a tear from her eye. "All right," she replied quietly. "You got it. You are my friend. I guess you always have been and always will be."

He gave her a weak smile. Weakness looked odd on the man who sat beside her, and she was unsure how it made her feel. "Thanks. It really does mean a lot." He reached into his blazer and pulled out the flask she had glimpsed earlier.

Jenny set her still full glass on the table and reached over to place her hand on his. "As your friend, I say, no more drinking tonight. You still have to drive home."

He sighed and returned the flask to his pocket with clear reluctance. Jenny was certain he would be drinking from it later, but at least she had been able to forestall him at the moment.

"I'll tell you what," she said with a slap on her leg, "I'll get us some coffee going. Would you like a ham and cheese?"

"Do you remember how I like it?" he asked.

She laughed. "Double ham, double cheese, three lines of mustard on white, of course," she replied as if she was reading back an order he had given at a restaurant.

This made both of them laugh, and she gathered up the wine glasses and headed back to the kitchen. After pouring out the rest of her wine in the sink, she started the coffee and then began making his sandwich. She said a silent prayer thanking God for bringing Mark back into her life, because, at this point, it was clear he was right—he really did need a friend.

What she wondered as she finished up his sandwich was if, in fact, what she needed was Mark as a friend, as well.

***

Mark pulled up in a parking space at Hopes Crest Church. Since it was a weekday, there was only one other vehicle there, an old pickup truck, and he smiled when Dave get out of it.

The door hinges ground as Mark opened the door of his own truck and he winced. His head was pounding from the hangover he had woken with this morning. Though he had sobered up at Jenny's the night before, as soon as he got home he had torn into a bottle of rum and today he was paying the price.

"Do you mind if we eat out here?" Dave asked as he handed Mark a fast-food cup of Coke. Then he dug into a brown bag, pulled out a burger and held it out to him.

"Sounds good to me," Mark replied, reaching up to take off the sunglasses, but changing his mind as the glare of the sun pierced his brain as sharply as an icepick.

Dave lowered the tailgate of the truck and they each took a seat.

"I'll tell you what," he said with a mouth full of burger, "Kayla's diner has the best food in the state."

Mark nodded absently. The burger was helping with the hangover, and his vision began to clear a bit, though he still kept the sunglasses on. "I appreciate you meeting me," he said after washing down another bite of burger with a swig of Coke, "especially on such short notice."

"Not a problem," Dave said with a smile. "It's my job. So, what's going on, my friend?"

"Well, you know Jenny and I used to date?"

"Sure, you guys were the perfect high school couple; the stuff movies are made of."

Mark chuckled. "That's an understatement," he replied. "Well, I really messed it up, our relationship, but she finally forgave me and I'm happy about that."

"That's good," Dave said.

Mark shrugged. "But it's like I still feel guilty about it. I keep seeing her on prom night in my mind. The tears, the hurt on her face. It still devastates me."

Dave sat quietly for a moment before he responded, and Mark wondered if the man was even listening. However, then Dave let out a sigh. "Have you prayed about it?" he asked.

It was not what he had expected to hear, but he should not have been surprised, since Dave was the pastor. "No," he admitted. "I mean, like I said before, I haven't been praying a whole lot lately. And, well, I wonder…" He allowed the words to trail off.

"You wonder if you have been away so long that maybe God stopped listening?" Dave finished for him.

Mark nodded, surprised that the man knew what he was trying to get at with his jumbling of words and ideas. "That's exactly what I'm getting at."

Dave set his burger on top of the wrapper on the tailgate. "He's there, all right," he replied. "No matter how bad we mess things up, He never leaves us. It's kind of crazy, huh?"

Mark laughed. Dave was so not the stereotypical pastor, which made him that much easier to approach.

"So, like in other relationships we're in," Dave continued, "if we stop talking to the other person, we feel that divide and it widens over time."

"That's it!" Mark said, glad Dave had pinpointed the issue perfectly. "I feel like I'm so far gone that maybe I need to start over again. Not just with God, but with Jenny, too. I mean, I've ignored God for the past four years, and that's bad enough. How can I ask Him for help when I've not bothered to go to Him in so long? Then, with Jenny, she at least accepted my offer of friendship, but I still love her, so I feel like I want more when she's made it clear that she doesn't."

Dave nodded. "Okay, let's review what you just said. You have two relationships going on you're worried about; one with the Lord and one with Jenny."

"Yes, that's right," Mark agreed, feeling excitement that maybe Dave would have a suggestion on how to straighten out his life.

"You're kind of talking to one, which is Jenny, but you're afraid to let go of the hurt you caused her, and at the same time, you want her to still be in love with you. Am I right so far?"

Mark nodded. "Spot on."

"Then, on the other hand, you know Someone who can take that hurt, someone who can forgive you and guide you, but you're reluctant to take your issues to Him because you're worried He won't listen."

Mark nodded again. "That about sums it up, I guess." He finished off the last of his hamburger, wadded up the wrapper and threw it in the bag. "So, what do I do now? See, I still love Jenny, and in my heart I want her back, but I don't know if it will happen or not."

"You mean you can't see the future?" Dave asked. Mark chuckled but did not reply. Dave gave him a wink as he hopped off the tailgate, waited for Mark to follow suit, and then closed the bed of the truck. "Look, talk to both of them, God and Jenny. Let them know your heart. I'm not going to lie to you, though."

"Please don't," Mark insisted. "I can handle the truth."

"Good. I know God is there and waiting to hear from you, that I have no doubt about. He will never forsake you.

With Jenny, though, I don't know how that's going to turn out, but keep her in your prayers. God will take care of that, but remember, it will be by His will, not yours. You have to be willing to accept how He answers those prayers."

Mark took a minute to digest what Dave was saying. It made a lot of sense. "I appreciate that," he replied. Then he felt his face heat up; he was not looking forward to the next part. "What about my drinking? It's really starting to bother me."

"Good," Dave replied firmly as he clapped Mark on the back. "It means you know it's not what you need. Every other Wednesday night at the library, there's a meeting for people struggling with addiction, including everything from gambling to drinking. The next meeting is next week. Do you think you might want to give it a shot?"

Mark thought about it for a moment. The thought of talking about his problems in front of a bunch of people really bugged him, but something inside told him to take the chance anyway. "What time?"

"Seven sharp," Dave said. "They'll even provide some food."

Mark laughed and followed Dave inside the church. And for the first time in a long time, he felt as though there was a direction for his life.

## *Chapter Ten*

Jenny looked over the small crowd that stood before her. Today was their first game and they would be traveling to Silver Ridge, another small mountain town which was an hour's drive away. The girls wore their new cheer uniforms, royal-blue with white lettering across their chests. The boys stood beside the girls in their white jerseys with large blue numbers and blue shorts. Both groups teemed with school spirit. Even some of the girls wore blue and white ribbons in their hair.

Mark stood beside Jenny, and she could not help shooting him a quick glance. He wore his blue blazer today, and Jenny was not sure why, but his hair looked really nice, not the tousled mess it usually was.

A snicker from one of the girls had her turning back to them. "As I was saying," she continued, sure she was as red as ever, "we will travel to the game today as a team and return as a team. The boys will sit together on the left and the girls on the right. And please, go easy on Mr. Herbert; he's getting older and we should show him even more respect than we typically would." She was happy to see the teens nod their heads in agreement. "Anything you want to add, Coach?" she asked as she turned to Mark.

"You heard Coach Jenny," he replied. "No funny business on the bus. You all have a job to do this evening and I expect you to be on your best behavior. Now, can I have our two captains step forward, please?"

Sam Brady and Kyle Rogers moved forward. The two had been dating for over a month and Jenny had assured Kayla she would keep a close eye on them on the bus. That was how she had come up with the idea of separating the teams; whatever she could do to keep the youngsters apart she was sure would be helpful.

"Your job is to keep an eye on your teammates," Mark continued. "Any problems, come to me or Coach Jenny." Both teens nodded their understanding. "All right, everyone, grab your stuff. The bus rolls out in fifteen minutes."

It was as if a race had started as both boys and girls rushed over to grab bags and purses. What began as whispers turned into near yells and loud laughter by the time they reached the doors.

"So, Molly had to miss the first game?" Mark asked as he walked next to Jenny.

"Yes," Jenny replied with a sigh. "She's just gone through a divorce and had to take off to Denver to fill out more paperwork." She glanced over at Molly's daughter. "I know Emma's heart is broken her mother couldn't be at her first game, but she's taking it all in stride."

"That's too bad about the divorce, but I'm glad Emma's handling it relatively well," Mark said. "Hey, wish me some luck tonight. I don't know why, but I'm a bit nervous."

Jenny laughed. "Good luck," she said firmly, "but you don't need it." She reached down to pick up her duffel bag from the bleacher. "You always bring good luck wherever you go." She felt her cheeks flush as he grinned.

"I appreciate that," he said. "All right, are we ready, Coach?"

Jenny nodded and the two headed out of the gym and into the parking lot where a brand-new silver bus sat waiting for them. "It looks like a rock band tour bus," she said with a laugh. What she had expected was either a yellow school bus or perhaps even an extra-large van, but the Montgomerys had insisted on giving only the best when it came to their daughter. Perhaps Jenny had been a little harsh in her previous thoughts on Louise Montgomery.

"Yeah, it does," Mark replied. When all of the students had gotten on the bus, Mark stopped and bowed. "Ladies first."

Jenny laughed and gave him a mock curtsy. "Thank you, kind sir." She made her way up the short but tight steps and glanced down the aisle. Sure enough, the boys and girls were already seated, but they were oddly quiet and Jenny found her suspicions growing.

"Hello, Miss Jenny," William Herbert said in greeting. The man was pushing seventy-something and wore large-framed glasses and his trademark woolen hat. Jenny had known him for years, like many others in Hopes Crest. Some said he had been driving students to school for so long, he used to take them in horse-drawn carriages. However, he was as good a driver now as he had ever been. Only the best drivers could navigate the twisting and turning mountain roads and still make their passengers feel safe.

"Hello, Mr. Herbert," she replied. "It's good to see you again.

The older man stood up, a look of shock on his face. "I can't believe it," he said in a loud voice as he looked past Jenny. "Mark Davis! It's good to see you, son." He extended his hand and Mark took it and gave him a firm handshake. "How've you been?"

"Fine, sir," Mark replied. "Thank you for asking."

"Well, you two take a seat and we'll get going." He pointed a gnarled finger at them. "And no making out like you used to in the back of the bus."

Jenny just about died from embarrassment as laughter broke out throughout the bus. A couple of girls grinned at her and one gave her a thumbs-up while the rest snickered and spoke in hurried whispers. She then glanced back at Mr. Herbert, and when she saw the huge grin on his face, she realized the girls must have put him up to it.

"I got this," Mark whispered when she had not moved. He moved past her, raised his hands up in the air and waited for the students to quiet down. "Okay, everyone, we're heading out. Are there any questions before we leave?"

A boy in the back row raised his hand.

"Yes, Paul?" Mark asked.

"You can have my seat if you two need some privacy," he stated. Another round of laughter rang through the bus and Jenny forced a smile as she turned to Mr. Herbert.

"We can leave now," she said. Then she walked down the aisle, counting heads as she went along, turned at the back and returned to the front, counting a second time to make sure she had the correct number of students. Then she took a seat beside Mark. "Everyone's here.

Now, if we can make it through the next hour, we'll be fine." She leaned back into the cushioned seat and raised her eyes to the roof.

"I think they got it out of their system," Mark assured her just before the sound of kissing noises and laughter came to her ears.

All she could do was groan.

***

"Attack, Attack, Attack," the girls yelled in unison as their pom-poms twirled and the visiting families cheered. It was the end of the third quarter and the Silver Ridge Bobcats were up by eleven on the scoreboard.

There was a two-minute break before the next period started, and Jenny glanced over at Mark. Immediately she knew something was wrong as he stood there staring at the scoreboard, his hand slapping the clipboard against his leg.

"Sam, keep the girls going," Jenny called over her shoulder. "I'll be right back." She hurried over to Mark as an announcement was made about the nachos on sale at the refreshment stand.

"Hey, what's wrong?" Jenny asked, coming up to stand next to him.

Mark turned toward her and she could not help but notice that his knuckles were almost white as they clutched the clipboard. "I think we're going to lose unless something changes," he said in a tight voice. "I shouldn't've taken this job."

Jenny put her hand on his shoulder. "What are you talking about? You're a great coach, and the kids love you. They look up to you."

"That's the problem," he replied, his eyes wide with fear. "They see me as a winner, but if I lose this game, they're going to hate me."

Jenny had never seen Mark like this before. She wasn't sure what was going in his head, but glancing up at the scoreboard, she only had a minute to try and help him. "You are a winner, Mark," she insisted. "And it goes beyond that scoreboard. If you guys lose, you lose as a team. You know that. Now, get over there and tell them what they need to do. Don't let fear get the best of you."

She worried he had not heard a word she had said, but when the warning buzzer sounded, he narrowed his eyes and said, "You're right. We can do this." He then ran over to the team, if not with complete confidence, at least with a little more vigor than he had when she first approached him.

Jenny went back to where the girls were waiting patiently to start their next routine. When she glanced back over at Mark, her heart went out to him. Where was the strong, confident guy she had once known? Though he no longer clutched the clipboard in his hands, he still appeared frail and broken, and the sight bothered her more than she cared to admit.

When the buzzer sounded again, Mark called out plays from the side. Jenny turned back to Sam and she gave her a nod, and the girls went into a new routine. The girls cheered as the boys played their game, and when the buzzer went off fifteen minutes later, Hopes Crest had lost by six.

Jenny's heart sank when she saw the look of pain on Mark's face as he shook hands with the opposing coach. She had known winning meant a lot to him, but his reaction to their loss was unreal. Letting out a sigh, she turned back to the girls, who were already getting their stuff together.

"All right, ladies, great job tonight. Let's hurry and get on the bus so we can get home." She then walked over to Mark, who was gathering up his stuff. His face was red and his jaw clenched.

"Hey," she said, and he looked up at her.

"I knew it," he grumbled. "I knew we were going to lose." He stuffed a water bottle into his duffel bag as if it had done him some sort of personal harm. "It was dumb of me to try to coach basketball. I'm going to hand in my resignation tomorrow."

Jenny pursed her lips. "Mark, don't talk like that," she said, but he just shook his head.

"I'll see you on the bus."

Jenny watched as he stomped off, sadness overtaking her. Glancing up, she looked at the gym lights. Why did so much hurt in both of their lives always take place in a gym? Whatever the reason was, she knew it was going to be a long ride back home.

***

The last parent had picked up her child, and Jenny stood leaning against Mark's truck in the parking lot of the school. Mark reached into his jacket pocket and pulled out the flask.

"Mark," she said quietly. "Are you sure you want to do that?"

"Just a little," he said before taking a swig and returning the flask to his pocket.

Jenny did not know much about alcoholics, but she had her suspicions he was one. Yet, how did someone approach it? She knew confronting him would not help much because she had already done that last week. One thing she did know was that she had to tread carefully. He had been quiet the entire trip back from Silver Ridge, but she hoped he would open up now that they were alone.

"You know, you can't win every game," she said in an attempt to reassure him. "It's okay to come in second."

He snorted. "That's easy for you to say," he snapped. "I was always pushed to be first."

She shook her head. "You don't think I was pushed by my mom?"

"You?" he asked in surprise. "What? How?" his brows were scrunched in confusion and Jenny could not help but understand. She had never told him in all those years they had been friends, or even while they dated.

A breeze picked up, moving a few leaves across the pavement, and Jenny shivered from the cold. Mark took off his blazer and went to drape it over her shoulders, but then stopped when she gave him an unsure look. "Go ahead and wear it," he said. "Plus, you can keep that flask from me."

"Thanks," she said as she slid her arms into the sleeves. It reminded her of when she used to wear his letter jacket back in high school. Then she once again leaned against the truck and crossed her arms over her chest. "So, my mom, sweet Mrs. Lana Hunter…" she continued and then changed her voice to mimic her mother's. "Jenny, don't eat too much or you're going to get fat.

Make sure you look your best. Don't frown or you'll get wrinkles. Stand up straight. Keep a smile on your face at all times; let everyone believe your life is perfect at all times." She turned to Mark. "Yeah, it wasn't always fun hearing that. Do you have any idea how many times I wanted to have even a little bit of ice cream or a slice of pizza and ate a salad instead? I can still hear her voice when I go to eat junk food, even if I haven't had it in over a month."

"Why didn't you ever tell me?"

She shrugged. "Probably the same reason you never told me about your dad," she replied. "I guess when you're young and in love, you skip over the important stuff."

He nodded as he crossed his arms and leaned against the truck. "Thanks for sharing that with me," he said as he kicked at a stone with the toe of his sneakers. "It means a lot."

She smiled at him and placed her hands in the pocket of his coat, her fingers touching the cold metal of the flask within. "Mark, why do you drink?" she asked, honestly wondering what his thinking was behind his actions. She hadn't been drunk many times, and when she had, she hadn't liked it all that much. "Why do you feel the need for it?"

He shrugged. "I don't know," he replied. "I mean, it's the pressure of everything on my shoulders. I can't take the weight at times, you know? So, when I drink, I don't feel it as much. It makes me numb so I can forget my problems, even if it's only for a while, if that makes sense."

She nodded, knowing all too well the weight one could carry on their shoulders. She turned to him and took his hands in hers. "But we both know there's someone who can bear that weight for us," she said quietly.

"I know," he said with a sigh. "It's been so long, though." Then he looked up and tears rimmed his eyes. "Can you pray for me?"

"I'd love to," she said with a smile. Then, underneath the night sky, Jenny said a prayer aloud for him, and though some would pray for a miracle, or maybe for some sort of sign, Jenny simply prayed from her heart.

When she was done, she opened her eyes and looked into his.

"Thank you," he whispered. "You know, there's a meeting for people with addictions at the library Pastor Dave told me about every other Wednesday. I know you have your own life and all, but I was wondering…"

"I'd love to be there to support you," she replied.

"Really?" His voice conveyed his shock.

"Yeah. That's what friends do; they support each other."

## *Chapter Eleven*

The folding chair Mark sat on was hard and wobbly, but he did not care. At least he was there. The group meeting was held in the small public library located on the block behind the arcade, right next to the post office, and Arnold, the group's leader, was making an announcement.

Mark knew a few of the eight people who were in attendance, and he had to admit he had been nervous when he first arrived; how would people look at him once they found out he struggled with alcohol? However, he had slowly acclimated himself to the group over the past hour as different people shared their stories of addiction that were in some ways so much like his.

He glanced over at Jenny. She had no idea that her being there meant the world to him. To know that he had her support was so important, he could not have even put it into words.

"Mark?" Arnold said, apparently not for the first time.

"Sorry," Mark replied. "What was that?"

Arnold smiled an easy smile. "No pressure," the man said, his thick graying hair combed back away from his face. "If you'd like to share something, you're welcome to. If not, that's fine, too. And remember, everything shared here is kept confidential. We're all in this together."

Mark glanced at a poster that hung on the wall behind Arnold. He had looked at it several times over the course of the meeting, and he found it resembled his own struggles with the picture of a mountain climber hanging off the side of a cliff.

"I don't mind," he replied finally. "I used to be popular around here because of my ability to play baseball. I got us to the state championships for the first time ever." A few people nodded their head. Of course, they would remember, everyone seemed to, which made what he had to admit even more discomforting. "I tried to make a career in Hollywood instead of pursuing baseball like everyone expected me to. The truth is, I really wanted to become an actor, but I also knew it was something I could do that was as different as it could be from what my dad wanted me to do." He shrugged. "I have to admit that what I did get to do when I was out in California, I enjoyed."

Arnold leaned forward. "Did your drinking start when you were out there?"

"It did," Mark replied, feeling as if his face was on fire. He could not look at anyone as he spoke, but he could feel everyone's eyes boring into him, especially Jenny's. "It didn't really become a problem though until about six months ago."

"What happened six months ago?"

Mark forced his jaw to relax, still staring at the poster on the wall. "That's when I decided to return to Hopes Crest. I needed to face some of the things I had done." He was speaking mostly to Jenny, but he wasn't going to tell her that in front of everyone. "I hurt someone really bad, and it tore at me. Though I've made amends with that person…" His voice trailed off and his heart felt heavy.

Then he glanced down as Jenny grabbed his hand and gave it a squeeze. In that hold, he felt his strength return and he straightened his back and continued.

"I'm having a hard time forgiving myself, but I've been going to church and getting my spiritual life back in check." Mark looked up and gave the group a weak smile, which was returned by several wide smiles, and at least one wink of encouragement.

Arnold was one of those who gave him a smile. "Mark, your story is not unique in the fact that not facing problems can lead to heavy drinking. The good news, however, is that we are here to support you. Do you have a support friend? Someone you can call on day or night when you feel at your weakest?"

Mark shook his head. Though Jenny had offered to accompany him to this meeting, the last thing he wanted was to add more of his problems on her. They had barely become friends and he was already blown away by her kindness.

"He does," Jenny answered for him as she gave his hand another squeeze. "Mark knows he can call me anytime."

Mark stared at her, unable to speak. It was amazing how such a beautiful woman had such a kind and forgiving heart that knew no bounds. It was a trait he admired deeply, though in the past he had taken for granted, and he made himself a promise to not ever hurt her again.

Arnold stood up and looked around the group, who also stood and then took the hand of the person next to them until a complete circle was formed. "It's been a great evening," he said. "I'm so glad to see how everyone has continued on his or her path to healing. We are so happy to have our new arrivals join us, and know that you have others here for you. To you all: Stay encouraged, stay grounded, and most importantly, stay in touch with each other. I will see you all in two weeks."

The circle broke after this and Mark turned to see Jenny smiling widely. "I'm proud of you," she said. "It took a lot of courage to say what you did."

"Thanks," he replied, his cheeks once again feeling warm. He was sure he had to be bright red. "I appreciate you being here for me. It means a lot." He looked into her eyes, eyes he could become lost in if he let himself. The truth was, not only did he miss her after all these years, he still loved her. If he could go back in time and do it all over again, he would. That night at the prom, he would have gone to Katie's party and then everything would have turned out differently.

"Look," Jenny said, "I better get going."

He looked down and nodded. They were still holding hands, and when she pulled hers away, he felt as though some sort of connection with her had been broken. "Let me walk you to the car," he said.

She smiled and waited as he said goodbye to Arnold, promising he would return for the next meeting. Then they headed out into the night air, chilled by a light wind that came off the mountain peaks and whistled lightly through the trees.

"So," Jenny said as they walked along the sidewalk, "big game Friday night. Are you ready for it?"

He nodded. "We've got a really good chance," he replied firmly. "And this time I'm not going to let fear stop me from doing my job." They turned to walk down the sidewalk that ran beside the post office and Galaxy Video and led to Elm Street.

"I'm glad to hear that," Jenny said. "Have you been praying?" She looked over at him and he did not miss the single raised eyebrow.

He shook his head. "You know I can't lie to you with that look."

They came to a stop once they reached Elm Street, and she put her hand on her hip and gave him one of her infuriating pouting looks. "And what look is that?" she demanded.

"That one!" he said, laughing. "Do you know how many times you gave me that look when you wanted to know something and I wouldn't tell?"

She tapped a finger on her lips. "Let's see," she replied and took a moment to pretend she was thinking. "I would guess easily a few hundred."

This brought on a burst of laughter from them both, and for a moment Mark thought that perhaps he had gone back in time, a time when they were both happy, and all he wanted to do was pull her into him, hold her, and let her know how much he loved her. She continued to smile as the two looked at each other, and feeling brave, he summoned up a tiny bit of courage that was well-hidden in his belly.

"You know," he said cautiously, "after the game Friday, would you like to grab something to eat? Just to celebrate, of course." He added the last in a rush with his hands raised as if to defend himself from whatever onslaught she might give him for even suggesting such a thing.

"I'd love to, but I have a date with Doug again," she said with clear dismay.

Mark thought his heart could not sink any lower than it had already, but it did, almost to his toes. He had forgotten she was dating, but other than that, they were just friends. He grasped onto that thought as if it was a lifesaver. "Of course," he said with a forced laugh, "I forgot about him."

Jenny cleared her throat. "Well, you should ask Cindy out again," she said as she turned to walk past the shops on Elm Street, many of them already closed.

"No, thanks," he said firmly. "I told you before, she's not my type." He wanted to add that Jenny was the only who was his type, but he kept that to himself instead. She was not ready to hear that just yet, he was certain.

When they arrived at her truck, she unlocked the doors with her key fob. "I'll see you tomorrow at school," she said as she opened the door.

"Hey, Jenny," Mark said before she could get into the truck. She stopped and turned toward him. "Thanks again for everything. The friendship, the support at the meeting tonight and at the game. I hope you know I appreciate it."

"I know you do," she said. She slid behind the steering wheel and a moment later she was backing out of the parking space.

He stood staring, hoping for a wave or even a smile, but she didn't give him even a second glace. Scolding himself, he headed over to the park across the street. His life was a mess, he was struggling with alcohol, and he expected her to give him a second chance?

As he sat down on the bench, he reached for his flask but then stopped. The temptation was great, but he knew he had to start taking small steps. So, he removed his hand and was glad it was empty of the flask, but sad it was empty of Jenny's hand.

## *Chapter Twelve*

Jenny bit at her lip as she pulled into the driveway, glad to finally be home. She had to fight the urge to turn and wave goodbye to Mark because she feared that would have set off a deluge of tears.

So many emotions ran through her heart, as many as the thoughts that surged through her mind, that she felt even more confused than ever.

As she entered the house, she went to the kitchen and smiled when she saw Katie wearing her usual long purple t-shirt that came down to her knees. Katie called it her relaxing pajamas.

"Hey, you," Katie said. "How did the meeting go with Mark?"

In her hand she held a spatula, which she was digging into a square baking pan. The aroma of chocolate wafting around the room told Jenny what was in the pan.

Brownies. Now if Jenny could keep herself from eating them all, she would be all right.

"It went well," Jenny replied as she plopped herself onto one of the stools in front of the island counter. "He made a lot of progress for his first night, I think. But besides that, yeah, it went well."

Katie smiled at her and then placed another brownie on the plate. "All right," she said in a firm tone, "we are going to have some girl talk time."

"What?" Jenny asked in confusion. "I don't need to talk about anything."

Katie snorted. "Oh, yes, you do," she said as she placed the now empty baking pan in the sink. "Now, go and change into your pajamas and meet me in the living room in five minutes."

Jenny knew better than to argue, so she headed to her room and changed into her shorts and a tank top. Then she pulled her hair back, grabbed a scrunchie off the dresser and wrapped it around her hair.

She took a glance at herself in the mirror and then paused to smile at the photos attached to the frame. Many of the pictures were from her high school years, several of her in her cheerleading uniform.

The way she and Mark talked tonight at the corner by the video store, laughing and enjoying each other's company, was like stepping back into the past, and that was what was reflected in those photos.

Her eyes moved over the pictures and stopped on one of her in her blue prom dress. The night Mark hurt her, walked out on her and left her guessing for years what had gone wrong.

It took her several moments before she could pull her eyes away from the photo, but she could not live in the past. She considered taking the pictures down and putting them in a photo album; she was getting a little old for photos stuck to her mirror.

However, before she could remove even one, Katie called out to her, "Hey, are you coming?"

Jenny pulled her hand away and stared at her collage one last time before heading back to the living room. She could not help but smile when she saw that Katie had set two large pillows on the floor, a few of their stuffed animals arranged around them. Next to Jenny's pillow, just as Katie's, was a glass of milk and a brownie.

"Sorry, I was daydreaming," Jenny said as she lowered herself onto one of the pillows. "Wow, I remember doing this when we were like…twelve? Thirteen?"

"I think even up to fifteen," Katie said, making Jenny laugh. "I must say, I do make the best brownies, though."

Jenny took a bite and then washed it down with a bit of milk. "You won't hear me argue."

"Okay," Katie said as she settled herself on the floor beside her pillow. "Now that my superb cooking skills have been recognized, what's going on, girlfriend? I know something isn't right. It's all over your face."

Jenny set her glass down and considered her friend's words. "It's kind of silly saying this," she said slowly, "but I'm confused about my feelings for Mark." She sighed. "Like tonight; I was happy being there with him, to support him, but he asked me to dinner. I mean, I'm not like exclusive with Doug, but I can't see Mark, not after all that happened with us before." She looked up and gave Katie a beseeching look. "What do you think?"

"Well, let's talk about Doug in a minute," Katie replied in a serious tone. "Let's talk about Mark first. So, he comes back to town, and of course, old feelings rise up; that's inevitable. You two have too much history for them not to."

Jenny nodded. "Exactly."

"So, what's stopping you from dating him again?"

"That's easy," Jenny replied with a sneer. "He walked out on me on prom night. Did you forget picking me up in the parking lot?" She could not stop the defensiveness that rang in her voice.

"Hey, I'm just trying to help," Katie said in a soft voice.

Jenny felt guilty for her tone. Why was she getting angry? Especially at Katie? The poor woman was right; she was just trying to help. "I'm sorry."

Katie waved a hand at her. "It's okay," she said, "but I thought you said you forgave him for that night."

"Well, I did, but I'm not going to forget what he did."

Katie grabbed her glass and drank the rest of her milk before turning back to Jenny. "Why not?"

Jenny gave her friend an incredulous look. Had Katie lost her mind? "Because he hurt me badly. I still want to…" her voice trailed off. She looked at Katie, who gave her a single nod.

"You want to strangle him? You want to let him know how badly he hurt you and maybe make him pay for it?"

Jenny felt the tears well up in her eyes and did her best to blink them back. "It's like…I'm so confused. I have every reason not to give him another chance, but I found myself tonight wanting to."

Katie laid a hand on Jenny's arm. "Honey, I know it hurts, but why do you think you're struggling with it? That was so long ago."

That was the million-dollar question, wasn't it? Why was she having such a hard time with Mark's return? For so long she had waited for him, despite her anger and humiliation. And yet, now that he was here, she found it all almost too much to bear. But in all reality, she knew the truth behind her confusion. "It's because he might do it again," Jenny explained. Then she shrugged. "It really doesn't matter; I have a date with Doug on Friday, anyway."

Katie pulled herself up from the floor, grabbed a box of tissues from a side table and handed a few to Jenny. Jenny did not even realize she had started to cry.

"Now let's talk about Doug for a minute," Katie said. "Let's be honest; there's nothing between you two, is there?"

Jenny sighed. "No. I mean, we both like pizza and…um…he…well…" She racked her brain to come up with some other commonality they had, but nothing came to mind.

"And there wasn't with Jason, Eric, or any of the other guys you went out with." It was a statement rather than a question. "And I think I know why."

Jenny stared at her expectantly. *This should be good,* she thought, *because I'm not even sure what's going on.*

"It's because you don't want to meet someone you might like. Honey, I think you've been purposely setting yourself up with men you have nothing in common with, maybe hoping that one day Mark would come back to Hopes Crest and you two would be together again."

Jenny nodded, the tears rolling down her face. Her friend's insight was amazing. "Doug is cute in that nerdy kind of way," she said, though saying it that way made her come across as arrogant, and she hated that. "I mean, there's nothing wrong with that, right?"

Katie smiled, put her arm around Jenny and pulled her in for a hug. "No, sweetie, there isn't," she replied. "Why don't you do this. Go out with Doug on Friday and see how it goes. If you want to continue seeing him, then by all means do it. But if you want to take a chance on Mark, then do that. It's up to you, and I will support you no matter what you decide."

Jenny sniffed and wiped her nose as she sat back up. "Thanks," she whispered.

She felt better and more clear-headed. It was really pretty simple; she needed to either commit to Doug or let him loose. It was not very fair of her to drag him along if there was no chance of them becoming a couple. She was not that kind of woman; never had been, never would be. "I don't deserve a friend as good as you," Jenny sighed. "You know that?"

Katie kissed her cheek and then stood up. "I do know that," she replied matter-of-factly, making Jenny smile. "You clean up the dishes. I need to get to bed."

Jenny hugged Katie once more and soon she was in the kitchen, putting the dishes in the dishwasher and wiping off the counters. As she worked, she made plans for how she would handle Friday night. She would have to make a decision between two men, but it was not only her decision to make.

As she lay in bed sometime later, she prayed for guidance from God, who would help her make that decision.

***

The next two days flew by, and before she knew it, Jenny found herself at Alfonsi Italian Restaurant seated across from Doug. The restaurant had the typical Italian-American décor with paintings of Italian landscapes in several spots on the textured plaster walls and ornate wine bottles used as flower vases on the tables. Soft violin music played in the background and the lighting was turned down low for the dinner service, to give the place a romantic air about it.

The boys' basketball team had lost again, this time with their first home game, and Jenny felt bad, not only for the boys but for Mark, as well. She could tell by his posture that the loss had affected him considerably, but he had sworn up and down that it had not. A shower and a quick change of clothes—a blue sweater and jeans, so nothing fancy—had been all she could manage to get in after the game, and she still showed up five minutes late for her date.

"The lasagna is really good," Doug said as he pointed down at the large square portion before him with his fork.

Jenny glanced at the indigo and white polka dot tie he wore and smiled. He was cute, there was no doubt about that. "It is," she replied. "I love the blend of cheeses." She took another bite to prove her point.

They sat in silence as they continued to eat, and Jenny found her mind begin to wander. Was Mark doing okay at the moment? He certainly had not looked well after the game, and she worried he would use his disappointment as an excuse to drink. Well, she could not focus on Mark at the moment. Later she would have to give him a quick call to check in, but for now she needed to concentrate on Doug.

"Is everything okay?" Doug asked as he set his fork down and wiped his mouth with a napkin. "You seem really distracted."

"Oh, I'm fine," Jenny replied with a smile. "So, any big plans this weekend?"

A waiter stopped by and refilled their water glasses before leaving them alone again.

Doug shook his head. "No, not really. I did manage to score some tickets to the Denver Symphony Orchestra in Denver in two weeks." He shot her a big smile. "I'd pay for a hotel room." He raised his hands up, although Jenny had not moved to make any comment. "Let me clarify. I will pay for each of our rooms. I'm not like that, of course."

Jenny held back a laugh. He really was a sweet man, and she did really like him, but not in that way. "I know what you meant," she said. "Would that be a Friday night?" When he nodded, she sighed. "I have games for the next six weeks, and they all are on Fridays. I can't miss them."

"Oh, of course," he said with a short laugh. "I totally forgot."

They returned to eating, and Jenny thought about the concert. She would not have minded going, to be honest, though she had never seen a live orchestra before. The problem was, she was not interested in going with Doug. She felt bad; the man was beyond nice, but there was simply no attraction to him. Especially compared to Mark.

Perhaps she should never have called Doug back. She did not want to hurt the guy, but she could not get Mark out of her mind.

"I wonder what I should do," she whispered to herself.

"What's that?"

"Oh, nothing, Mark," she said absently before taking another bite of her lasagna.

Doug smiled at her with a slight shake of his head. They went quiet again and Jenny forced her mind to focus on her food, but her attention kept being pulled away by images of Mark and the look of defeat after the game. There had to be something she could do to help him, but she could not think of anything that did not include them spending more time together than was prudent.

Ten minutes later, after they had both finished the rest of their meal in silence, Jenny was surprised when Doug asked for the check.

"Do you have to be going?" she asked as she pushed back her chair and stood. "We could grab a coffee if you'd like. I'll even buy." It was strange. Usually they would spend some time talking, and she watched in wonder as he quickly counted out the money for the check.

"Thank you, but no," Doug said curtly.

She scrunched her brow but said nothing as she followed him outside and headed toward her car. Something was definitely wrong. "Doug, wait," she said as she threw her coat over her shoulders. "Did I do something to upset you? I'm sorry about the concert; I would've loved to have gone."

"No, Jenny," he said with a heavy sigh. "You called me Mark. That was your ex's name, right?"

She lowered her head, guilt washing over her. She did not even remember doing it. "It is," she replied quietly. "I'm so sorry. I have been all over the place with work and stuff." She gave him a weak smile. She knew what decision she had to make when it came to whether she and Doug should continue dating; the answer was no.

Then a thought hit her. Of course! What if there was no chemistry between them because of Mark's return? She had been so focused on that man the last few weeks that she had not given Doug a second thought.

He was cute, had a great job, and even went to church. What if she was throwing away something good?

She was reminded of a movie she and Katie had watched not long ago, and the way to find an answer to her problem was quite easy.

"If you'd rather," Doug started to say just as Jenny leaned in and planted a kiss on his lips. His eyes widened significantly and Jenny felt her heart sink. There was nothing there. "Grab a coffee," he said, finishing the sentence he had started before the kiss.

The look of confusion on his face brought forth a feeling of regret in Jenny. She took his hands in hers and shook her head. "I'm sorry for that," she said earnestly. "I needed to check something."

He nodded and gave her a weak smile. "Nothing, huh?"

She shook her head. "To be honest, I've been having confusing feelings over Mark, and at this point, I just can't date anyone else for now, even you."

He shrugged. "It's okay. I mean, you have to follow your heart, and well, I still think you're a beautiful woman. I really do hope it works out for you, but if for some reason it doesn't, would you give me a call?"

Jenny nodded, let go of his hands and then hugged him. "I promise that you will be the first person I call," she said.

When the embrace broke, Doug smiled at her again. "You take care," he said. "And good luck."

"Thanks."

Jenny slid into the driver's seat and leaned her head against the headrest. God had made it pretty clear that Doug was not the man for her, but now it was time to find out if Mark was the one. She pulled out her phone to turn back on the ringer and saw she had received more than one text from Mark.

'I know you're on your date, I hope you're having fun. I'm sorry for being rude earlier. I was having trouble dealing with the loss. I've been tempted to drink, but I won't.'

Another text followed. 'I'm actually feeling way better. No temptation to drink. Can't wait to tell you why.'

She hit reply and typed in, 'I'm so glad. I have some good news to tell you, too. Call me when you get a chance.'

She returned the phone to her purse and went to close the door of her truck when she spotted Mark's truck parked across the square. There were only a few places open at this time of night, one of them being The Outlaws, the local bar.

"Oh no, Mark," she mumbled as she got out of the truck and hurried past the closed salon just a few doors down and to the bar. Country music blared as she opened the door and walked inside. The place was packed, or at least Hopes Crest packed.

She looked around the crowded bar and did not spot him. Then she stopped dead in her tracks when she caught sight of a familiar blazer on the dance floor, the owner's back to her. The woman dancing with him moved until her smiling face appeared in one of the overhead lights. It was Cindy Peterson, the same woman Mark had told Jenny just a few days ago that he had no interest in.

Cindy moved in closer to Mark and ran her hands across his back in a seductive manner and a moment later, the two embraced and kissed.

Jenny's stomach twisted as she headed back out of the bar and ran to her truck. Tears of anger clouded her eyes as she started up the truck. Why had she believed she and Mark still had something there? She had mistaken his reaching out in friendship as something more, and now the humiliation crashed over her in waves.

Driving down Elm Street, Jenny's hands tightened on the steering wheel. She had made a fool of herself with Doug not only half an hour ago, and now she was back to no one to date and stuck working with Mark. That thought made her press the gas pedal that much harder.

## *Chapter Thirteen*

Mark stood next to his truck in the school parking lot with his hands in his pockets and his spirits low. They had lost their first home game, and that was bad enough, but to top off the night's events, he regretted being rude with Jenny earlier. He moved his gaze up to the dark sky; the stars were out in full numbers tonight and the field was lit up by them.

"Hey, Coach," a voice called out, causing Mark to turn around. He smiled when he saw Robert, Kyle's father, walking toward him.

"Hey, Robert," Mark replied. "How are you?" He offered the man his hand, and Robert took it and gave it a firm shake.

"I'm good. Hey, good try tonight. The boys are getting better." He did not even sound sarcastic.

Mark shrugged but gave no reply.

"No, they are," Robert insisted. "I can see it. I might have some ideas that might help out, if you're interested."

"Oh, yeah, I forgot you coached them last year, didn't you?" Mark said. He gave a half-hearted snort. "You wouldn't want your old job back, would you?"

Robert laughed, running a hand through his dark gray hair. "No thanks," he replied, still chuckling, "but I can go over some things with you next week when I pick up Kyle from practice. He's grounded from driving for a month, except for work." He shook his head. Kyle was also the local pizza delivery guy.

"Oh, that's too bad for him," Mark said. He did not feel right in asking what Kyle had done to be punished. "But, anyway, that sounds great. I could use the help. I feel bad for the boys; they're giving one hundred percent and I've been letting them down."

Robert's brow crinkled. "Hey, you win as a team, you lose as one. Don't be so hard on yourself. You're a hero around here for a reason; you always come out on top in the ninth inning, or in this case, it'll be the fourth quarter."

Mark laughed. He appreciated the man's kind words, and as he thought them over, he found himself feeling quite a bit better about the whole situation. It was true; he did always come out swinging hard when the odds were stacked against him. "I appreciate that," he said in all honestly. "It means a lot."

"It's only the truth, so no problem," Robert replied. "Look, I'd better get back to Kyle, make sure he knows what chores he has to do tomorrow. I'll talk to you later." Then he turned and headed back to his car.

Mark made his way toward the baseball field, a lighter bounce to his step. As he walked, he sent Jenny a text; he had already sent her one earlier, and it was not very positive. He certainly did not want her worrying about him, especially since she was on a date.

'I'm actually feeling way better. No temptation to drink. Can't wait to tell you why.'

He returned the phone to his pocket and thought of Jenny for a moment. He could not imagine her with any other man, but with Doug it was even more surprising. The guy just was not her type, or so Mark thought. Then again, people change. Apparently, the man made her happy, and though it crushed Mark to know she was eating dinner with the guy, he was happy she had found someone she seemed to care for.

The baseball field had not changed one bit in the past four years, and he smiled as he walked over to home plate. He closed his eyes for a moment and remembered that game four years earlier. It was as though he could still feel the first pitch fly past him and the umpire's yell of "strike!" carry across the field. With his eyes closed, he made a solemn vow; just like when he was in baseball, his coaching would be no different. He would work extra hard with the boys, and even if they did not go far, he'd make sure he gave it his all. It was not all about winning, after all.

"Davis steps up to the plate," he said in his best announcer's voice. "The Warriors are only two strikes away from ending their dream of becoming the State Champions." Then he lifted an imaginary bat up and over his shoulder. "The pitch is a junk curve, and...Davis swings!" he pulled his arms around to swing and then put his hand up to his forehead as if shading his eyes from the sun. "It's going...it's going...gone!"

He laughed as he jogged toward first base. He could still hear the crowd's roar. As he made his way around second, he imagined rounding third and seeing his teammates waiting at home plate.

Jenny would be there, too, just like she had been that day, and after celebrating with his teammates, he and Jenny would embrace tightly.

However, as he made his way around third base, someone else stood at the home plate.

"Bravo!" Cindy shouted with a laugh as she clapped her hands together. "I don't think it even landed." Her very tight black jeans and light pink leather jacket seemed almost out of place in the dark field, and Mark wondered why she was there.

"Thanks," he said, the weight of embarrassment crushing down on him as he stepped on home plate. "I'm just reliving the glory days, I guess. What are you doing here?"

"My niece and family came to watch the game tonight, and I came with them. You didn't see me in the stands?"

"Sorry, I didn't," he replied. Why would he have even been looking for her? They began walking toward the parking lot. "So, what did you think? The team isn't too bad, are they?"

She laughed as she patted his arm. "Not at all. You're doing a great job with them. But, then again, you are Mark Davis. I know you will make them all winners."

Mark was unsure how to respond, so he simply replied with a quick "Thanks" as he attempted to hide the bit of skepticism that still clung to him. "That's kind of you." They approached his truck and he stopped before opening the door. "Well, it was good seeing you again, Cindy, but I should go."

"Wait," she said as she grabbed his arm. "Tonight they have a country band playing at The Outlaws. I was wondering if you'd like to go."

He offered her a small smile. "I'd love to, but I'm cutting back on my drinking. It's not the best place to be when you're trying to stop."

"That's crazy," she said with a shocked look on her face. "I've been cutting back myself. I could use someone there to make sure I don't give in to temptation. Would you mind being that person?"

Mark felt conflicted. He really did not want to go and be tempted to drink. Plus, he had no interest, romantically at least, in Cindy. But the way her eyes were pleading, he found it hard to say no. Maybe she really needed the support, and who better than a person struggling with the same issue? He could go for an hour or so; a bit of dancing would be nice and it would not be that bad, especially if she needed as much of a boost as he did.

"All right," he conceded finally. "Then…"

She cut him off. "Awesome!" She ran around the truck and said, "Let's go then; I'm going to need a ride."

Mark shook his head and got into the driver's seat. "How did you know I was going to go with you?" he asked. "If I'd have said no, you would've been stuck here." He turned down the radio, put the truck into drive and drove through the parking lot to the entrance.

"Mark, you're too much of a gentleman to just leave me here," she replied.

He laughed as he pulled out onto the street. "So, what's new?" he asked, trying to relieve the silence that surrounded them. "I'm surprised you're single."

She giggled and pulled a strand of her blond hair behind her ear. "Tell me about it," she replied. "I'm just as surprised as you are." She crinkled her nose into a grimace. "There's really no one to date around here, and I'm not going to lower my standards and date someone from Silver Ridge." She shrugged. "What about you and Jenny? I thought you two might be getting back together."

Mark slowed down as they neared the Town Square. "It's complicated," he replied. "I mean, we're friends and all, and she's dating someone but it's not serious."

The truck slowed and he turned onto Elm Street.

"I see," she said. "Well, that's good. I hope it works out for you two."

Mark smiled as he pulled into an empty parking space across the square from the bar. As he got out of the truck, he wondered what Jenny was doing at this moment and if she was still on her date.

"Hey, Mark," Cindy said as they started to walk across the street.

"Yeah?"

"I hate to be the bearer of bad news," she said as she nodded toward Alfonsi's.

Mark followed her gaze and his heart sank. Jenny and Doug were talking just outside the restaurant doors and, much to his horror, they moved in for a kiss. It was not exceptionally long, but it was still a kiss.

"It looks like it's pretty serious," Cindy mused.

Mark nodded in agreement and then watched as the two held hands. Cindy was right, Jenny and Doug's relationship was much more serious than he thought, and he felt his heart drop. Any chance he might have had with Jenny was over.

"Come on," Cindy said as she slipped an arm through his and pulled him toward the bar. "We can still have fun, right?"

He nodded absently and allowed her to lead him through the park and across the other side of the square. He glanced over one more time at Jenny and Doug. The two were now in an embrace. Though he felt crushed, he hoped she was happy.

The Outlaws bar was packed and Cindy took his hand in hers. He hoped she was not getting the wrong impression, because even though there was no chance with Jenny, Mark still had no interest in Cindy. She was a good-looking woman, to be sure, and would turn any man's head, but he felt absolutely no chemistry with her.

"Now," Cindy shouted to be heard over the blaring music and collection of voices, "You're going to dance with me and smile." She dragged him to the dance floor and began to wiggle her hips in front of him.

"All right," he sighed. "I guess I will." He forced a smile at first, but as he moved to the music, he found his smile becoming slightly more genuine.

There was no point in being down, and moping over Jenny would only lead him to hitting the bottle, something he did not want to do. His hands went to Cindy's waist, and she smiled at him.

"You know, I have to be honest," she said as she leaned in to shout in his ear. "I always had a crush on you."

He smiled. "I kind of wondered," he replied back. "I remember a few times you'd smile at me in the hallway at school or during some of the games." They moved around to allow a waitress to pass them, and Cindy put her hands on his back.

"I couldn't help it," she said as she moved in closer to him. "I was so jealous of Jenny, but when I heard you were back in town, I just had to try to see if I could get you out with me."

Mark laughed. He could not help but admire her openness. "Well, thank you. I'm flattered. But I want you to know, I like you as a friend, and at this point, I'm not looking to date anyone."

Her eyes narrowed for a moment and then her smile widened as she looked past him. He went to glance over his shoulder and her fingernails traced across his back.

"Cindy," he started to say, but the next thing he knew she was kissing him. She just planted a huge kiss on his lips while her hands pulled him toward her. He was so shocked, it took him a moment before he realized what was happening and he pushed her away. "I'm sorry, but I have to go."

"Wait," she called after him. He stopped and turned around to face her again. "Look, I'm sorry. Please stay?" She grabbed his hand and pouted at him. Even though he was not with Jenny, his heart still was, and he felt horrible for the kiss he and Cindy had just shared, although he knew it was more her kissing him than the other way around.

"No, I'm sorry, but I can't," he replied. "You can get a ride home, right?"

She nodded, but there was clear reluctance in it, and then she walked away, heading to the bar. Not once did she look back at him.

Mark took a deep breath and wound his way through the crowd to the front door. Once outside, he pulled out his phone.

He smiled as he read over the text he had received from Jenny. She wanted to talk to him, and that made him very happy. He dialed her number and leaned against the wall as he waited for her to answer.

## *Chapter Fourteen*

Jenny rubbed her temples as she sat at her desk and then glanced over at the silver cross, that symbol of hope she had received as a gift all those years ago. At this moment, all she hoped for was to get this paperwork for new equipment completed, especially before the girls began cheer practice for the day. However, she was finding it difficult to concentrate, and that really was not like her at all.

The office door opened and Molly walked in. "Hey, Jenny," she said with a half-smile on her face, "I hate to bother you, but do you have those forms completed yet? Linda's asked me five times, and each time she seems just a bit more agitated than the last."

Jenny sighed. "Yeah, give me a second. I'm almost done."

She added a few more notes, stacked the papers together and jabbed them into the electric stapler. After the sharp *click,* she handed the pages to Molly. "Tell her I'll talk to her later if she has any questions."

"Okay, I will," Molly replied before turning back around to head out the door. She stopped in the doorway and turned back. "Not to be nosy or anything, but are you okay? You look kinda tired."

Jenny nodded. She had not slept well the past three nights, since her date with Doug had soured and her mixed feelings over Mark had hit her like a ton of bricks. "I'm fine," she said with a heavy sigh. "I just need more sleep. But hey, by the way, thanks for the help. I'd be going crazy right about now without you here."

This made Molly smile broadly. "Thanks, and I'm glad," she replied. "Let me get this to Linda and then I'll set out the mats for practice."

Jenny waved her away but continued to stare at the closed door in wonder. She knew the woman was going through her own issues, including a recent divorce, but how she managed to keep smiling was beyond Jenny. However, when she glanced over at the silver cross, she had a suspicion as to how.

"Lord, help me figure out my feelings," she prayed silently. Then she grabbed her whistle off the desk. It was not fair to Molly to be stuck preparing for practice, so rather than sitting in her office sulking, Jenny would go out and help.

However, before she even got around her desk, the door opened again and Mark came walking in. Jenny stopped dead in her tracks; she had hoped she'd figure out some way to not have to bump into him today, at least not while they were both alone.

"Hey, there you are," he said in a joyful voice. "I've been trying to call you. I didn't see you at church yesterday. Are you doing all right?" Like she did with Molly, Jenny wondered how Mark could smile so much. However, a vivid picture of him dancing with Cindy and their kiss on the dance floor helped answer that question.

"I'm fine," Jenny replied curtly. "I need to get going."

Just as she pushed past him, he grabbed her arm. "Wait, please," he begged before releasing her arm. "What's going on? I know when you're upset. Is there anything I can do?"

She spun around and placed a hand on her hip. "Nothing is going on," she snapped. She took a deep breath to calm her nerves and then added in an only slightly calmer tone, "Why do you ask?"

"Well, you aren't responding to my calls, for one."

"I went out with Doug again," she replied, though it was a lie.

He winced almost imperceptibly, and Jenny clenched her jaw. The same old Mark, wanting the best of both worlds. He probably expected her to dump Doug to go out with him, but she should be okay with him still dating Cindy? Granted, she had already broken it off with Doug, but he did not need to know that.

"Oh, really?" he asked.

"Yeah," she replied. "And it was so romantic. That man, I tell you, he knows how to charm a woman."

He stared at her for a moment, and then looked down at the floor. She grinned. He was a good actor because he had almost fooled her, but she knew what she had seen at The Outlaws. "It's getting serious between us," she continued. "Who knows, maybe he'll pop the question soon."

Mark's head snapped up. He stared at her for a moment and then said, "Well, good. I hope he's the right one for you." He shifted uncomfortably. "Oh, hey, good news on my end, too. Robert, Kyle's dad, is going to give me some coaching tips."

"That's nice of him," Jenny said through gritted teeth. She was surprised that Cindy had not offered to help, but she would not put it past the woman to show up today.

Mark was still smiling, but barely. "Yeah, it is nice of him. Hey, you said in your text you had good news. What was it?"

Jenny bit at her lip as she searched her mind for a way to reply. She hated to lie, but he seemed happy to be with Cindy and it really was unfair of her to get between them. "It's not important," she said finally. Lying never came easy for her anyway. Then she thought back at what she had said about her and Doug and she cringed inwardly. Maybe it did come easier to her than she thought.

"You know, I was thinking that, after the game Friday, maybe we could grab some coffee together. Of course, bring Katie along, too, and we'll all go out like old friends."

Jenny shook her head. It would not be fair to put either of them through all that anymore. "I think she's busy," she replied. "Look, I need to be straight with you."

He crossed his arms over his chest and leaned against the desk. "Okay, go on."

She steeled herself for another lie; oh, how she hated it. "With Doug and I moving forward, and with the past you and I share, I think the friendship needs to end. It's just not right."

"I see," Mark said, a clear look of sadness spreading across his face. How she wanted to give him an Oscar, his performance was that good. "You're right, and I apologize for that. So, strictly professional from now on?"

Jenny nodded. However, hearing the words aloud hurt after what her heart had gone through on Friday. There had been that little bit of hope that they would have been dating by this week. Instead, she was trying to find ways to keep them apart. That was what needed to happen.

"I respect that. Can I ask you one thing though?" When she nodded, he continued. "My meetings. The next one is still ten days away, but I'd still love your support."

Jenny's mind spun around in circles. What she needed most was to keep as far away from him as possible, especially on a personal level, but she also knew that his drinking was not a part of his act. She felt like her heart was being torn in two as she mulled over what she should do.

However, before she came to a decision, Mark raised a hand to her. "You know what? It's cool. I can ask someone else."

"No," she burst out. "That's fine. But just that." What she wanted to do was turn around and beat her head against the door. It was not like she was his only friend in town; he had many. So, why did she feel the need to be there for him for this? Well, it was too late now; she had already committed. "Anyway, I have to get going. Have a great practice, Coach. I'll see you around." And with that, she walked out the door.

It took every ounce of energy to maintain a steady pace, but she made it to the gym without incident, where Molly was already setting out the mats for practice. Jenny had thought that, once she told him there was no possibility of a relationship, she would feel a sense of relief. However, she found with each step she took, she became that much sadder.

## *Chapter Fifteen*

Mark glanced up from the small desk in the office, his eyes resting on Jenny. For the past five days, she had barely spoken two words to him, and it was driving him insane.

He understood that, now that she was in a serious relationship with someone, they could not go out together, even as friends. But to completely cut him out of her life was not something he would have expected from her.

Sighing, he returned to the notes he had taken the previous night when Robert had stopped by after practice. They had spent over an hour in the gym and Mark had picked up quite a few tips he was hoping would help them at tonight's game.

They would have the advantage since it was another home game, and he felt confident that they might actually win this one. In fact, over the past nine days, his confidence had grown exponentially as the number of days he stayed sober had grown.

The greatest contributor to his increasing self-assurance, however, had to be attributed to his increased prayer life. The first few prayers had been pretty bland as far as prayers were concerned, but then he pushed aside the bravado and simply told God what was on his heart.

By doing that, he felt better and the lines of communication widened. Now, if he could only get the same friendship started again with Jenny.

He remembered the conversation with Pastor Dave about how talking to God was like any other relationship—that is, you just needed to talk—

so he figured that the only way to bridge that rift between him and Jenny was to simply open his mouth. Yet, he could not get himself to take that step.

"Will you stop banging that pen!" Jenny snapped. She wore a dangerous scowl, and Mark considered for a moment that she might leap at him.

"Sorry," he mumbled, dropping the pen on the desk. "I get lost in thought sometimes and then next thing I know, I'm annoying people." He gave a half-hearted laugh, but she ignored it, instead going back to the paperwork on her desk. "It should be a good game tonight," he said in a feeble attempt to somehow open up that line of communication. However, she did not even look up from her work. "Pine Bluff is winless, like us, so it sounds like an even match."

Jenny set her pen on the desk and turned toward him. "That's great," she said, though it sounded forced. "I hope you win."

Mark swallowed. Now that she was looking at him, he was not sure what to do next. Perhaps he should just say it. "You know, you seem on edge lately. Is there anything I can help with? Are you and Doug okay?"

She leaned back in her chair and laughed. "We're fine," she replied. "Thanks for asking. I don't know why you'd care, though."

He shrugged. If she only knew how much he truly cared, but there was still too much of a roadblock between them for him to say as much. Plus, it would not be fair to Doug. "I still view you as a friend," he said. "I just want to make sure you're fine."

Jenny stood up and grabbed her notebook and whistle. Mark was pretty sure it was wrong of him, but he could not help but still find her amazingly beautiful, even when she was mad. No, especially if she was mad.

"I'm fine, Mark. Look, I need to meet the girls. Good luck tonight." Then she shuffled between the desks and walked out of the office.

Mark let out the breath he had not realized he was holding and gathered his clipboard and notes. He glanced over at the silver cross. A few weeks ago he would have been in despair, but now he knew there was hope, and even though they would just remain friends, at least they would begin to talk again.

***

With twenty seconds left in the game, Mark glanced up at the scoreboard. The game was tied and the noise was deafening, feet banging on the bleachers and hands clapping while the crowd screamed and cheered. The cheerleaders had worked overtime getting the crowd excited, and it had paid off. The energy in the stands was unreal.

"Okay, Brandon," Mark said as the boys huddled around him, "I want you to throw the ball to Paul. When the clock gets to seven, Kyle, you wait behind him for the pass. Take it to two seconds and then shoot. The rest of you, make sure you stay on your man. Everyone got it?"

The boys around him nodded, their bodies and faces covered in sweat, but their smiles wide.

"Are we gonna win, Coach?" Paul asked.

Mark made eye-contact with each player before responding. He knew the looks they had on their faces because he, himself, had seen and expressed the same before. It was the look of wanting the coach to assure them that everything was going to be just fine.

"Yeah," Mark replied. "We are going to win it." The warning buzzer sounded and he stuck out his hand. "Come on, hands in." Each team member placed his hand on top of the hands already there. "On three." A moment later, they all yelled, "Team!" in unison and then broke the circle.

Holding the clipboard across his chest, Mark glanced over at Jenny, who was looking right at him. He offered her a smile and she turned away.

The ref blew his whistle and Paul did exactly as Mark had instructed him, dribbling the ball with an opposing player close but not suffocating him.

The crowd got louder, if that was possible, and Mark found his heart beating faster as the clock ticked. Right as it hit seven seconds, Paul faked an advance right as Kyle moved in behind him.

"Now, Kyle!" Mark shouted, hoping his voice could be heard over the screams of the crowd.

Kyle faked right and dribbled left. Just as the clock dropped to two seconds, he jumped up from the three-point line and soon the ball was flying in a large arch. It was as if time stood still, and then the ball dropped straight into the basket.

If the crowd had been loud before, it was excruciatingly so now.

"We did it!" Brandon shouted as Mark rushed the court. All the boys ran in together and embraced each other and patted each other on the back.

"I'm so proud of you all!" Mark yelled, emotion coursing through him. Soon people from the stands were pressing in around him, all cheering and congratulating the team. Mark shook several parents' hands and then glanced over to see Jenny standing apart from the crowd.

Mark jogged over to her. "Hey, thank you," he said sincerely. "The way your girls got the crowd worked up, we couldn't have done it without them. And you."

"I appreciate it," Jenny replied with a half-smile. A thousand thoughts went through Mark's head, but then he heard someone call his name and he turned to look over his shoulder. He could not tell who had called him, there were just too many people, but the person could wait. Jenny, however, did not agree. "You probably should go, Coach."

He wished he could stay there with her, but she was right; he had his duties. "Yeah, I guess I should," he said. "I'll talk to you later, okay?"

He returned to the players and soon got caught up once again in all the excitement of winning their first game of the season. His confidence, as well as that of the players, was soaring, and once the celebration wound down, he wished them a good weekend. The group separated, each player going his own way. When the crowd had dispersed and he thought he was the only person left, he walked over to collect his things and almost jumped when he heard a voice behind him.

"Great job, Coach."

He turned and frowned when he saw Cindy walking up to him. She wore a dress that would have been considered much too short for a high school game; it clung to her body and showed off every curve, and he made sure to keep his eyes on her face.

"Thanks," he replied. "I think we're going to keep improving with each game."

"With you leading them, I know they can go far." She stepped in closer to him, making Mark feel uncomfortable, and when she placed her hand on his arm, he debated whether or not it would be rude to slap it off. "Why don't we go get something to eat?"

She wore that same pouty look she had worn at The Outlaws the previous week, and he wanted nothing to do with what she had to give.

"Cindy," he said slowly. He wanted to be clear, but he did not want to be rude either. "I've told you before, and I don't want to hurt your feelings or anything, but I don't want to date you. It's nothing personal…"

"Whatever, Mark," she snapped, the innocent, playful woman now gone. "You're still head over heels with Jenny. You know she's in a relationship now, right? It's over between you two and it's time you accepted that." She tilted her head and the pout returned to her lips. "Date me. It'll be fun."

He held back the urge to snort. "I'm sorry," he replied. "I can't."

She shook her head and crossed her arms over her chest. "Fine then," she said. "See ya around." And with that, she stormed off, her heels clicking firmly on the wooden floor.

He let out a sigh and then turned to see Jenny standing by a far door. He offered her a wave, but she simply shot him a stern glare, grabbed her duffel bag and hurried out the door.

## *Chapter Sixteen*

Jenny shoved open the double doors and headed toward her truck. Several families still dotted the parking lot and she gave a couple of them a wave, though her heart really was not in it. Her mind was on Mark and Cindy.

She could not believe the way Cindy had dressed for a high school basketball game, but that was Cindy. What really ate at her was the way Mark was ogling the woman; it was pathetic.

In all honesty, she could not blame him; Cindy had always been extremely pretty, and every boy in high school had wanted to date her. They still did, if Jenny listened to the rumors. The way Cindy used to smile at Mark back in school had been bad enough, but seeing the woman give him those same looks tonight demonstrated that she still would love to get her hooks in him.

Why would any of this surprise her? Mark could have any woman he wanted, and if a woman like Cindy was pursuing him, how could she blame him for wanting to go out with her? It was not like he and Jenny were seeing each other, so who was she to have some sort of opinion about it?

*Then why are you so angry?* she asked herself.

"Jenny!"

Jenny rolled her eyes and did her best to ignore Mark, who she could hear jogging up behind her. She opened the truck door and tossed in the duffel bag.

"Jenny, wait, please."

There was no way she could not have heard him, since he was now standing right behind her. She forgot how fast he could run.

"What?" she said moodily as she slammed the truck door and leaned against the side of the bed with her arms crossed and her lips pursed.

"Hey, what's going on?" he asked as he tried to catch his breath. "It's been a week and you're acting like I have leprosy or something. We should talk this out, whatever this is."

Jenny laughed. "There's not much to talk about," she replied. "Besides, you should get going, don't you think? Your girlfriend's waiting for you."

Mark gave her a blank stare. "Girlfriend?" A car passed them and honked and Jenny waved at the Canton family. Mark still stood there with that blank expression on his face. "I have no idea what you're talking about."

Jenny snorted. "Cindy?" she said as she pushed off the truck and reached for the door handle. "I've seen the way she looks at you. It's been the same since we were in school. And come on, her dress tonight? You were looking at her like she was a side of beef."

Mark laughed and shook his head, which only fueled Jenny's anger even more.

"Don't deny it! I saw you two dancing at The Outlaws last Friday, and then you were kissing right there on the dance floor."

For some reason, this made Mark double over with laughter. Jenny debated whether or not she should take his clipboard and hit him over the head with it.

"Oh, Jenny," he said between gasps, "you have it all wrong."

"Oh, really," she snapped as she placed her hands on her hips. "Amuse me, please. I'd love to see how you two making out is not what I saw."

He nodded as he wiped at his eyes and took a couple of deep breaths before speaking. "I was struggling with wanting to drink last week, you know, because of how bad the team's been doing."

This brought on a wave of guilt in Jenny. She was supposed to be the person he could call if he was struggling. However, she said nothing as she waited for him to finish his explanation.

"Then I found out Robert was going to help me with some coaching tips. That's when I sent you that text about feeling better; not wanting to drink anymore."

What he said made sense. "But what about Cindy? That was the second time you two went out on a date; well, that I know of, anyway."

"She asked me to go to The Outlaws with her. I didn't want to at first, but she told me that she had been struggling with drinking, too, and needed support. Since I felt like I was doing so well, I figured it was only right to help someone else who was in the same boat." He put his hand up defensively. "Yeah, I fell for it. She made the move on me on the dance floor, I swear. I suppose you didn't see me push her off of me, huh?"

She shook her head in response; there were no words she could think of at that moment that could have expressed how bad she felt. Of course, she had not seen that because she had stomped off like a jealous teenager.

"And you probably didn't hear me tell her that I had no interest in her at all tonight and how she stormed off after."

A flush went through Jenny's body. She felt horrible. All week she had treated him like dirt, ignored him, and lied to him, and there was no reason for it.

*Is there ever a reason for it?* she asked herself harshly.

"Mark, I'm sorry," she said in a quiet voice. "I guess…well, I was jealous." She found it difficult to look him in the eye as she admitted this. This was not the type of person she was, and yet, here she was, acting this way.

"Hey, it's okay," he said soothingly. "Things happen. But I'm still confused."

She gave him a hesitant glance and what she found were kind eyes and a warm smile greeting her. It made her heart soar; how she had missed him.

"Why are you so jealous of Cindy?" he asked. "I mean, you have Doug. I saw you two outside of Alfonsi's." He raised a single eyebrow. "That was a pretty heavy kiss."

Of course he had seen that. She gave her head a slight shake. "Well, I guess I'm not the only one who saw something that wasn't what it appeared to be," she replied.

She gave a heavy sigh and then explained about the disaster that had followed after their third date and finished with the experimental kiss. When she was done, she looked up at him expectantly, trying to gauge his response. Would he be disgusted with how she had used poor Doug? She knew she was.

"The thing is," she said when he did not respond, "I've been confused. I've been struggling because I want us to date again, but I'm scared about what happened before. I don't want my heart to be crushed again; I don't think I could handle going through that once more." A hot tear rolled down her cheek. "I'm sorry for lying to you this week. I'm so sorry for everything."

He stepped up and pulled her into his arms, and all the old feelings that she had carefully packed away since that night four years ago unraveled and rose to the surface.

"Of course, I forgive you," he whispered. "I'm so sorry for hurting you. I want us to date again, and I know I have a long way to go to prove you can trust me." He pushed her back lightly and looked into her eyes. "The question is do you want to take that chance?"

The doubt still lingered inside her like a bad chest cold, but she summoned up as much courage as she could, hoping that, the second time around, they might just get it right. "I do," she replied and found that she really did want to take that chance. "But let's go slow though, okay? I need some time to get rid of this skittishness I seem to have when it comes to us. Also, we need to remember that work needs to remain professional."

Mark nodded his head in agreement and pulled her into him once again. She put her arms around him and returned the embrace. How long they stood there in each other's arms, Jenny did not know, but by the time the hug broke again, their cars were the only ones left in the parking lot.

She glanced up into his face and smiled. She had not realized it, but they were standing directly under the very light post where they had broken up after prom. And now, four years later, the spot was a reminder that misery could be replaced by hope.

***

Jenny applied the last bit of makeup and gave herself a final look-over in the mirror. Though she had told Mark the previous night she wanted to take it slow, they had arranged to go out this afternoon and spend some time getting reacquainted. The clock on her phone showed just past noon; Mark would be arriving at any moment, and she was ready.

Katie walked up behind her and Jenny smiled at her friend's reflection in the mirror. "I swear, you are so nervous," Katie said with a smile as she leaned against the door jamb.

"Just a little," Jenny replied. "I mean, it is a date."

Katie rolled her eyes, and Jenny lightly slapped the woman's arm before following her into the kitchen. Jenny grabbed her purse off the table. "Do you think I look all right?"

Katie took a few steps back and tapped her finger on her chin. "Perfect hair, just enough makeup to enhance your natural beauty, light-blue sweater and blue jeans. I guess it'll work." She shot Jenny a wink. "You look wonderful. Besides, you've seen the guy almost every day since he's been back. What makes this so different?"

This made Jenny laugh, and then she covered her mouth. She felt giddy, as though this were her first date ever with the man, or any man. "I don't know," she said. "I'm excited, but this is our first real date since…you know, before."

"Well, have fun, but make sure he has you home by ten. I'm not going to allow late-night dating in my home." This brought on another bout of laughter.

The doorbell rang and Jenny squealed. "That's him!"

Katie groaned. "You think?" She walked over and gave Jenny a hug. "Love you, and have fun, okay?"

Jenny gave her a quick nod and then went to answer the door. When she opened it, her smile grew.

"Hey, Jenny," Mark said, looking handsome in his dark blue sweater with white lettering of the school team embossed on the front. Jenny could not help but assess him; his smile, his hair, his eyes—the list could go on forever—were all perfect.

"So, are you ready?" he asked, still standing on the stoop.

How long had she been staring at him? "Oh, yes, of course," she replied with a laugh. She closed the door behind her and followed him to the driveway where his truck was parked.

When he opened the door for her, she said, "Why, thank you, sir," which made her giggle.

Then he replied, "But, of course, madam," which made her laugh even harder and by the time he slid behind the steering wheel, she had tears running down her face.

"I didn't think it was that funny," he said as he started the truck and gave her an amused smile.

"It wasn't really," she managed to eke out. She waved a hand at him weakly. "I don't know. Just drive." It was almost painful trying to get her laughter under control, but when he responded with "But, of course, madam; your driver does as you say," she completely lost it.

He joined in her laughter as they made their way down the road. When they could finally breathe once again, she asked, "So, what's the plan?"

He gave her a sly smile and flicked his thumb toward the back seat where a picnic basket and blanket lay.

"Oh, a picnic lunch?" she said in admiration. "Aren't you the romantic?"

"I try," he replied. "I have to be honest, I was a bundle of nerves this morning. Both excited and nervous, do you know what I mean?"

Jenny shook her head. "No, not at all," she replied but followed it up with a giggle. "Well, if you're going to be honest, then I guess I should be, too. I have to admit that I was the same way all morning."

He turned onto Parker Road and Jenny tried to figure out where they were heading. When the truck slowed down and turned into the parking lot of the school, she looked over at him in surprise.

"The school?"

"Well, the field, to be more precise," he replied.

Jenny smiled as he pulled the truck up into a space close to the baseball field and a moment later they were walking up the sidewalk that led to the green.

"I know it's nothing fancy," Mark explained, "but I figured it'd be cool."

"No, it's fine," Jenny said. She started to head toward the bleachers but Mark kept walking straight toward the field. When he got to home plate, he handed Jenny the basket and then flicked out the blanket and placed it right across the plate.

"There," he said as he took the basket from her, "now you won't get dirty."

She smiled and sat on the blanket. He followed suit and sat down next to her, the backstop behind them. Jenny looked over the baseball field as Mark began unloading the picnic basket.

"Okay," he said, "I made these myself." He handed her a sub sandwich on a paper plate and a small bag of potato chips.

"I'm sure it'll be wonderful," she said as she took the plate from him. She found it kind of cute and her brows rose in confusion when he handed her a Thermos.

"Purple, Kool-Aid," he said, and she laughed. Then he handed her a napkin and smiled. "We'd better pray."

She nodded and slipped her hand in his and bowed her head. After he said a quick prayer, she looked up to see him immediately tearing into his sub.

Unwrapping her sandwich, she took an experimental bite and then smiled. "Hey, not bad at all," she said. "There's hope for you yet." He held up a finger as he tried to chew quickly. "Men, never responding to women," she added with feigned annoyance.

"Hey, give a guy a break," he said once he had washed down his food with a bit of Kool-Aid. "I'm glad you like it, though."

She smiled as she opened her bag of chips. "So, why here?" she asked. "I'm not complaining, but I'm not sure I see the significance."

He shrugged. "My life, at one point, revolved around baseball and nothing else. Well, that's a lie, it revolved around you, as well, but baseball came first. I remember, after hitting that home run, jogging around the bases and coming back around to home plate and there you were, waiting for me. It's the fondest memory I have of baseball."

Jenny thought her insides would melt. That day she had not known his true feelings about the game, so it never occurred to her that she had affected him so strongly. The idea that he found her so important to him was kind and soothing to her soul.

She chuckled. "I remember rushing the field. The crowd was so crazy, and then there you were, walking over to me with that smile…" She shook her head. "Yeah, that was a special night for me, too." What a strange feeling to remember how important it had been to her that he had been so happy that day, especially after so many years of anger and hurt to cover it up.

It went quiet for a moment, the only sound the crinkling of a chip bag or the rustle of the paper that covered a sandwich as they continued to eat. Jenny's mind drifted thinking of different things from her past; many happy, a few sad. But none of it mattered now; Mark was back and they were giving it another chance.

"You know, this means a lot to me, this date," Mark said, breaking the comfortable silence that had fallen upon them. "I know we're taking things slow, but I'm excited. I think we still have something great, or that we can get it back. You know what I mean?"

Jenny nodded and turned towards him. She did know what he meant, and she felt the same.

She was not surprised when, in the back of her mind, that lingering doubt tried to break back into her consciousness. She pushed it back down with only a little effort this time. It was time to get rid of the past and allow the future to make its own path, and to do that, she would need to continue to pray that everything would work out just fine.

## *Chapter Seventeen*

The night of the second support group meeting at the library rolled around, and Mark smiled at Jenny, who sat beside him. The same faces from the first meeting began taking their seats around the circle, and Mark leaned in and whispered to Jenny, "I appreciate you coming."

"Of course," she whispered back. "I wouldn't miss it for the world."

Mark smiled again and sat up straighter. That was the thing about Jenny; she would give up everything to help someone out or be there for them. It was a trait he admired and respected.

A few more people sat down, and then Arnold looked around and smiled at the group. "It looks like everyone is here," he said. "I'm glad to see you all and I wanted to start tonight's meeting with some updates. Would anyone care to share anything?"

A woman, who appeared to be in her forties with dark hair specked with gray and pale skin, raised her hand. Mark tried to recall her name and was pretty sure it was Sally.

"Go ahead," Arnold said.

"Thank you," the woman said. "I've been struggling with drinking over the last month, and I finally gave in and decided one wouldn't hurt, would it? But just outside the liquor store, it hit me. Do I really need it? Was there something else I could do to take away the stress I'd been dealing with? So, I turned right around and went and bought a tub of ice cream instead." This brought a bit of understanding laughter from everyone, including Sally.

"That's great," Arnold said and then asked a few follow-up questions.

Mark listened to the woman's responses, and it was comforting to know that others struggled in much the same way he did.

When she was done, Mark decided it was time for him to say a few words. "So, I've been able to stay sober for two weeks now." The members of the group gave him words of approval, which surprisingly made him feel like a million bucks. "I'm finding the thought of reaching for my flask happening less often, but I've been praying a lot and spending time with a really good friend." He shot Jenny a quick smile, and she returned it easily.

Arnold smiled. "Mark, that's great news. What about your dreams of being an actor? Is that something you still might pursue?"

Mark noticed Jenny shift in her seat and clench her hands in her lap. He'd have to ask her about that reaction later. "You know, I had my chance at it, and it didn't go as well as I'd hoped. But that's okay. From now on, I'm just Coach Mark, and that's what I plan on doing for a long time."

Arnold leaned forward and clasped his hands in front of him. "That's good; you should be happy wherever you are. Do you ever see yourself doing something along those lines again? You mentioned last time that the drinking started when you realized the roles weren't coming to you."

Mark shrugged. "Not really, no. It's like you said, I need to be happy with where I am now, and I am."

Another member took his turn, and while he spoke, Mark looked at Jenny again. Her demeanor had changed, and Mark returned the weak smile she gave him.

For the remainder of the meeting, Arnold shared strategies for dealing with moments of weakness, as well as solutions for particular problems the members might struggle with.

By the time the meeting was over, Mark was feeling more encouraged than ever. As he mingled with a couple of the other members, Jenny walked up to him.

"I'll see you next time," he told the others before turning to Jenny. "I think I'm good for the night," he said, though she had not asked. "Thanks again for coming."

"You're welcome," Jenny said and she glanced down at her phone as they walked toward the exit.

Once outside, they stopped in front of her vehicle.

"I want you to know, that I'm proud of you. The way you open up, the struggles you're facing, you're doing great," she said.

"I appreciate it, but it's only been two weeks."

"Two weeks is better than no weeks. Now, where is that Mark Davis can-do attitude?" She poked him in his stomach.

Mark laughed. "Good point. I appreciate everything, Jenny. I hope you know that."

"I do. Look, I'm going to go ahead and head out to meet Katie. Do you need me for anything else?"

He opened the door for her and they walked out into the small parking lot where they had both parked. "No, I'm fine for now," he replied. "I guess I'll see you at school tomorrow. Have fun."

She put her arms around him and he returned the hug. "I will," she said. "I'll see you tomorrow." Once she had slid into the driver's seat, he shut the door and she started up the truck.

He watched her drive off, and he whistled as he headed to his own car. Everyone had their ups and downs, and now he was heading up again. Life was good, God was great, and nothing would ever separate the him from Jenny again.

Feeling renewed, he drove off and decided to head home for the evening.

***

Monday morning, Mark sat in the school library trying his hardest to listen to Linda Miller carry on about the schedule for the next few months for the entire school. He was finding it difficult to focus and wondered what all this had to do with him as a coach and phys ed teacher.

Apparently, because he was the phys ed teacher and thus an official member of the staff, he was required to attend, but it was times like this that he wished he could turn back the clock and decline the position. If he was just a coach, he would not have had to be here.

He glanced over at Jenny, who was in the same boat as him, and she smiled. Linda was a stickler for making everyone attend on non-student contact days. He remembered, as a student, loving these days when the teachers were forced to be at work while he got to sleep in late and enjoy his day off doing whatever he wanted. Now he only felt guilty for that joy.

Linda adjusted her glasses as she skimmed over the packet of papers in her hand. Greg Townsend, the history teacher who was sitting next to Mark, leaned over and whispered, "I'm going insane."

Mark gave him a quick nod. "Tell me about it. I hope we break for lunch soon."

Greg sighed and Mark turned back to Linda. Why she chose to make them wait in silence for so long between each point was beyond him; all it did was lengthen the meeting time.

Finally, she tapped the packet of papers on the podium before her and looked up. "Although I do not believe children at this age should be allowed to dance, powers above me have deemed it so. Our annual Homecoming dance will take place on the thirteenth of November, and I'm looking for volunteers to supervise it, as well as a volunteer to put together a group of parental chaperons."

Mark glanced around the room. The teachers all suddenly seemed to have found a sudden interest at something on their shoes or in a stack of papers in front of them. When he looked back up, his heart sank as his eyes locked onto Linda's.

"I'm sure our hometown hero would be happy to help," she said with a thin smile.

Mark swallowed hard as all eyes were on him. Greg whispered, "Thanks for taking one for the team. You'll be respected for your sacrifice."

Mark could not help but chuckle. "Sure," he replied. "Why not?" He tried not to laugh at the collective sigh of relief that resonated around the room.

Then Jenny spoke up. "I'll help, too."

Mark shot her a surprised, yet relieved, glance and she responded with a smile and a thumbs-up.

"Splendid," Linda said. "Well, that's all I have for our staff meeting. I'll dismiss us for lunch in just a few moments, but I wanted to let you know that I will be out for the rest of the day. I expect you all to work hard despite my absence."

Everyone around him nodded in agreement, and Mark shook his head. Linda treated them all as if they were school children.

It was like a stampede as everyone headed to the doors. Jenny walked up to Mark with a wide grin. "I forgot to warn you to look down," she said with a laugh.

"Well, at least you stepped up to help me again."

"That's what I do," Jenny replied. "I step up and help those I care about."

Mark's heart rate quickened at the words that soothed his soul.

"So do you want to grab something to eat?" Mark said, hoping she would say yes. His heart dropped for a moment as she shook her head.

"I don't know, I kind of wanted to get back to the school early and start on work." She paused for a moment then laughed. "You are getting to easy. Come on, you're driving and buying."

Mark smiled taking the car keys from her. "If I am buying then I get to pick."

***

Mark walked into the gym with a bag of food in one hand and two drinks in the other, hoping not to spill them. Coming up to the bleachers, Jenny sat down, crossed her legs and then smiled at him.

"Are you going to hand me my drink or make me take it myself?"

He laughed as he set the bag down, and then using his free hand, handed her the soda.

She thanked him as he came and sat beside her. "OK. So, before we eat your delicious meal of gas station hot dogs and nachos, we need to pray," she said.

He reached out and took her hand.

A moment later, he bowed his head and then she prayed. "Lord, thank you for the work you do in our lives.

Sometimes we go through so much and don't know why, but you do. So, I ask that you continue guiding Mark's and my steps, and that we do everything for your glory. Amen."

"Amen," Mark echoed and then opened the plastic bag and handed her the nachos, followed by a hot dog.

"Are you trying to get me fat?" Jenny asked with a laugh as she took the lid off the nachos. "If I get any bigger, you'll be running for the hills."

"What?" Mark said with a laugh. "You look great. I wouldn't care how much you weighed. You're perfect."

She smiled and then looked down at her food and began to eat. He wanted to tell her that she was perfect in every way, and it was the strength inside her that he cherished and, to be honest, loved. Instead, he took a bite of his hot dog and then looked over the gym. It was quiet now, and he thought back to watching Jenny cheer at the basketball games when they attended here, and then the night of the dance, which seemed like a lifetime ago.

"When you get quiet, it means you're thinking," Jenny said. "Which means trouble."

"Yeah, right," he said playfully. Then he grew serious. "I was just thinking of a girl who used to cheer here. She was a good-looking woman."

Jenny took a drink from her straw. "Is that so?" she asked. "What's her name?"

"I couldn't say," he said and then laughed as her fist hit his arm. "OK! Her name was Jenny! She was the best!"

"That's better," she said and then went back to eating.

Mark smiled. Their dating had been slow thus far, but even moments like this—eating cheap nachos and having a laugh—meant everything to him. He had messed up before and lost her, but he would never let it happen again.

## *Chapter Eighteen*

Kayla Brady lived in an exclusive part of Hopes Crest that had houses as large as mansions with its own private lake. Jenny had been there several times for various reasons, and she could not help admiring the views around her as she walked up to the front steps to Kayla's house.

The front porch had a homey feel about it with a two-seater swing and a rocking chair. That was one thing Jenny liked about Kayla; she might have a lot, but she was down-to-earth and one of the kindest people Jenny knew.

The basketball team had a bye week, so this left Jenny free to go to the monthly women's group meeting, which she loved. It had been a tough decision giving up the meetings for coaching, but she knew that if she did not take up the coaching, the school would be hard-pressed to find someone else who had the time to take it on.

The doorbell gave off a grand, melodious sound when she pushed the button, and Kayla opened the door only moments later, the echoes still resounding through the house.

"Hey, you," Kayla said, giving Jenny a hug before moving aside to let her in. "Thanks for coming early."

"No problem," Jenny replied. "Is everything okay?"

She followed Kayla through the foyer and down a hallway to the kitchen, which was located in the back of the house. The woman's kitchen was larger than Jenny's living room and kitchen combined with its granite top counters and double wall oven. Even the refrigerator was massive with extra wide stainless-steel double doors. Jenny appreciated what Kayla had, but she had never been envious.

Instead she looked it all as nothing more than a blessing for a woman she considered a good friend.

"Every thing's great," Kayla replied. "I just wanted to ask, or rather be the first to know, if the rumors are true." She had a knowing smile on her face, as if she already knew the answer.

Jenny laughed as she took the bottled water Kayla offered her. "Yes, Mark and I are dating again," she sighed dramatically.

Kayla's eyes glittered. "I know it's bad to gossip and listen to rumors, but I heard it through the grapevine and just had to know the truth." She leaned against the counter. "I'm happy for you, I really am."

"Thanks," Jenny said. "We're just dating, not quite a couple yet, so we'll see how it goes."

Her mind went back to a few days ago and the lunch with Mark in the gym. The way he had called her perfect with his goofy smile had brought such a joy to her heart she almost cried.

"Interesting, so my source was right," Kayla said with a grin.

She gave Kayla a suspicious look. "How did you know? Who told you?"

"Oh, hey, Coach Jenny," Sam said, giving her a flashy smile as she walked into the room.

"I see," Jenny said as she narrowed her eyes at Sam playfully. "No need to explain. I wondered if my cheer captain had been paying extra close attention to me lately."

Sam laughed and headed to the refrigerator. "Sorry," she said, though it was clear she was not really sorry. "You have to admit, though; you two look cute together." Jenny laughed, but Sam only grinned wider. "All right, I'm heading upstairs. See you in a bit."

When she was gone, Jenny turned back to Kayla. "So, what about the Brady household?" she asked as she twisted the lid off her water bottle. "From what I understand, you're seeing someone."

Kayla nodded. "I'm still with James, and let me tell you, he's the sweetest guy ever." She sat down on one of the stools and set her water bottle on the counter. "It wasn't easy at first. A lot was my fault, but it's been great since we ironed out all our issues."

"That's good," Jenny said honestly. She really was happy for Kayla. She remembered hearing about Kayla losing her husband while he was deployed—Jenny was in high school at the time—and the thought of losing someone you loved had to be devastating. Yet, Kayla had always shown a great strength that Jenny could only admire. "The few times I've talked to James, he seemed like a really nice guy."

"Yeah, he definitely is." Kayla sat staring off dreamily and then shook her head as if waking herself. "Anyway, there's another reason I asked you over early. I was going to talk to Dave, but what do you think about having a young women's group for the teen girls? We have more attending church every week, and I think it'd be fun. Plus, it would be a great way to guide the girls through this crazy part of their lives. What do you think?"

As far as Jenny was concerned, the girls could most certainly use a place to share and build each other up that did not include another activity to take away their focus, and Kayla would be great as a group leader. Too many teenagers lacked guidance in their lives. Not that she faulted the parents too much; so many had to work long hours just to make ends meet these days.

"I think that's a great idea," she replied. "But why do you need me?"

Kayla smiled as she pushed her red hair behind her ears. Jenny recalled that the woman had won a few beauty pageants years ago, and she could see why. She still had not lost any of her natural beauty. "The girls adore you," Kayla said, "just as much as I do." When Jenny went to say something, Kayla stopped her. "Seriously. The way they look up to you and respect you is out of this world. Assuming Dave comes on board, which I'm sure he will, what do you think? Do you want to help me run this group? I mean, you have a gift working with teens; you should use it in every way possible."

Jenny considered Kayla's proposition. On one hand, she loved being with the girls, and just like Kayla said, more and more teenagers were attending church services. This was a great idea considering the path of the rest of the world. Yet, as much as she loved working with the girls, there were times when they drove her crazy.

However, when she looked at Kayla's smile and her excited expression, Jenny could only answer one way. "Sure," she replied. "I'd be glad to help."

"Oh, Jenny, you're wonderful!" Kayla said, giving her a hug. "And not just because you chose Sam to be captain, mind you." This made them both laugh. "You know," Kayla added as she sat back on her stool, "we should go grab coffee sometime. We hardly ever hang out anymore."

Jenny smiled. "That'd be fun. I agree, we should do that."

The doorbell rang, the chimes louder now that Jenny was inside the house, and Kayla went to answer the door.

Her phone dinged, and taking it out of her pocket, she saw she had received a text from Mark.

'So, do you ladies sit around and knit at these meeting? I'm dying to know.'

Jenny laughed as she typed out her reply.

'I can't tell you. It's a secret. I'll call you later.'

She set her phone on silent and then put it away just as Kayla returned, followed closely by a small group of other women. Susan, Kayla's best friend and coworker had always been funny and very nice. Behind Susan was Dolores Van Schneider, who, of course, would never miss a meeting held by any group that had to do with the church. Despite the woman's forwardness, Jenny wondered if she was secretly lonely and used the church as a way to keep control over her life as a longtime widow. Sometimes she felt bad for thinking poorly of the woman, but then Dolores would say or do something that only solidified what Jenny thought of her.

By the time everyone had arrived, there were a total of seven women standing in the kitchen. Kayla set out fruit and vegetable trays and a stack of paper plates, inviting everyone to grab something to eat before they headed to the living room. Jenny found it interesting that Kayla would allow anyone to eat in such a grand room, but when Jenny mentioned it, Kayla just waved her off.

"Don't be silly," she said. "It's just a living room. Everything can be cleaned."

"Hello there," Dolores said, her nose held high, as it typically was. "Rumor has it that your boyfriend is dating a married woman and that was how you go the new bus."

Jenny glared at Dolores, realizing this was one of the reasons she found the woman so distasteful, but before she could call out a retort, Kayla stepped in to defuse the situation.

"Dolores," she said firmly but kindly, "you know that rumors like that are unfounded. Of course, it's not true."

Dolores gave a derisive sniff. "Perhaps not," she said haughtily, "but I was simply asking, nothing more."

As the older woman made her way to the living room where the other women had already gone, Kayla shot Jenny a look that said she found the woman insufferable before following.

"That woman is something else," Jenny whispered to Susan when Dolores was out of earshot.

"Tell me about it," Susan replied. "I think most of the rumors she hears she starts herself."

Jenny smiled as she took an empty seat and soon joined in one of the many conversations going on around the room. And though she tried her hardest to concentrate, she kept thinking of Mark and his goofy grin.

***

Mark took the last bite of his cheeseburger and then patted his stomach. He had to admit, A Taste of Heaven made the best burgers this side of Denver. How many times he had wished he could have one during his stint in California, he could not remember, but it was quite a few. Pastor Dave sat across from him, also enjoying a cheeseburger with as much vigor as Mark.

Betty, their waitress, set a new Coke on the table and picked up his now empty glass. "Free refills for the local sports legend," she said with a wink.

"Aren't there free refills anyway?" he asked amusedly.

She shrugged. "True, but I'm just buttering you up for my tip." She placed the check upside down on the table and walked away, her grin never slipping.

Mark grabbed it and waved off Dave, who had gone to reach for it as well.

"Well, if you insist," Dave said with a laugh. "This has been nice. Nothing wrong with having time for oneself once in a while, is there?"

Mark laughed as he pulled a few bills from his wallet and placed them and the check on the table. "I agree with that," he said. "So, you told me that when we were done eating, you had something to ask me. I'm all ears."

Dave wiped his hands on a napkin and then pushed his plate away. "I know you told me you were done with the acting thing, but are you really done?" Mark gave him a questioning look and he quickly added, "What I mean is what about a local production?"

Mark looked at Dave with interest. He had never considered anything local, at least not when it had to do with acting, but his curiosity was piqued. "Sure," he replied. "I mean, I'm done hoping on the Hollywood thing, so sure, how can I help?"

His love of theater would always be with him, he knew as much, but doing something in Hopes Crest definitely sounded interesting.

"Well, every year, the church puts on a Christmas play." Dave glanced around and then lowered his voice as he turned his attention back to Mark. "To be honest, the last few years since Geraldine passed, the acting has been…well, I guess you could call it 'stiff'. Don't tell anyone this, but even I fell asleep during last year's performance."

Mark laughed so hard, tears began rolling down his face. Dave was great, a real guy who laid it out on the table and never held back; not one of those stuffy men who acted as if they had never sinned and passed judgment on everyone else around them. It was one of the many reasons Mark respected him.

"I don't mean to disparage the work that was put into those productions, mind you, but it could use a more…skillful touch, if you know what I mean. The message will still be the same, of course, regardless of the production, but…" He let the words trail off.

"I get it," Mark replied. "When I shot that pilot for *Night Sky*, some of the actors...well, I had no idea how they were even able to audition. Of course, by the time we shot the pilot, the not-so-great ones were weeded out, but I get what you mean."

For a moment, his mind returned to Hollywood. The casting calls, the standing in line and waiting for hours to have a chance to read for a part. Then when he was selected to co-star in the police drama, he thought his prayers had been answered.

How quickly things could change.

"Well, you don't have to audition for a part," Dave explained. "But we could use some direction, a person with experience to help the actors get into character. What do you say?"

"Count me in," Mark replied readily, his mind already thinking of ways he could help. It would be fun, and maybe Jenny would be willing to participate.

"Good," Dave said with a relieved sigh, as if he had been uncertain whether or not Mark would agree. "We won't start rehearsals until after Thanksgiving, and the play only lasts about thirty minutes. A lot of the performance time is taken up by the choir."

Betty stopped by and collected their plates and the check.

Dave placed his forearms on the table and clasped his hands. "So, how are things overall?"

"They couldn't be better," Mark answered honestly. "I've been sober since forever now. Coaching is going great, and well, Jenny and I have started dating again."

"Oh, really?" Dave said with a look of mild surprise. "So, the rumor mill is true?" They both laughed at this. "In all seriousness, though, that's great. It looks like your prayers have been answered."

Mark smiled. Indeed, they had. Not only had his relationship with Jenny gotten back on the right track, so had his relationship with the Lord. It was a matter of priorities, and Mark had learned a valuable lesson.

The two men continued talking for a few more minutes and then parted ways for the evening. As Mark walked to his truck, he took out his phone and checked the messages. Seeing one from Jenny, he smiled and then dialed her number.

## *Chapter Nineteen*

Time flew by faster than Jenny could have ever thought was possible. Now, the second week in October, the boys' basketball team was playing what might have been their final game of the season.

It amazed Jenny how much they had improved since those first losses. They had continued to win up to this point, and though they had lost the first of a double game tonight by a single point against one of the top teams, they still gave it their all during this second game.

Their fate now rested on how this game ended. Win it and they would go on to the qualifying matches, which would last another month, or lose and hang up their jerseys for the season.

Thankfully, they had home court advantage, and the cheerleaders were working the packed crowd, which was on its feet clapping, shouting and singing. The noise in the gym was deafening.

Jenny glanced over at Mark, who was pacing back and forth shouting words of encouragement and commands, or so Jenny imagined since she could not make out what he was saying. *Can the players?* she wondered. However, it did not matter, they were playing the hardest she had seen them play all season, and she was proud of their perseverance.

It was not only the team that made her swell with pride. Mark had come so far in every aspect of his life that she could not help feeling even more proud of him. Not only had he abstained from drinking, his confidence in his coaching had surged to the point that, when they had lost that first game, he had nothing but praise for his team.

He had not allowed it to bring him down, and that was a major improvement on his part.

However, the greatest progress she had seen was in Mark's spiritual life, which had grown by leaps and bounds. Where he turned to alcohol when he had a problem, now he turned to prayer and Bible study. He was a completely changed person, and Jenny loved him for it.

It was that word, love, that had been plaguing her over the past week. She had told Mark in no uncertain terms that they needed to take it slow at the beginning of this rekindled relationship. Then it had been she who had seemed to dismiss it almost immediately. But she was willing to accept responsibility for accelerating their dating. Even though they continued to work together in a professional manner, she could not resist having him over for dinner or to watch a movie together.

The truth was, over the past month, she had fallen for him again, and she would be the first to admit it if anyone asked. Yet, she had not told him outright how she felt. Though the feeling was wonderful, a tiny seed of fear still resided deep inside her, a seed she continued to push away and discourage from growing.

He was setting up roots again in Hopes Crest, that much was clear, but she still could not let go of what he had done before. It was not fair of her to not trust him completely; perhaps it was not even true forgiveness.

Whatever the case might have been, she knew she needed to push past it and tell him how she really felt, and soon. Maybe if she voiced it, the fear would finally leave her and they could move on with the path that God had set before them. However, even as she considered revealing her feelings as she watched his pacing beside the court, the doubts crept in.

What if she told him how much she loved him and then he broke her heart all over again? The thought was nauseating, and looking at him, she found herself torn. Maybe she should hold off telling him just yet. There was no rush and that realization brought her a bit of comfort.

It was settled; they would continue dating, not make it too serious for the time being, and see how things went. That would keep them together to work on building a more stable relationship and protect her in the meantime. Her stomach settled at making this decision and the contented feeling returned.

"Coach Jenny?" Sam asked, breaking Jenny from her thoughts. "They aren't going to lose, are they?"

Jenny shook her head as she glanced up at the scoreboard. The boys were down by seven with just a minute left. "I don't know, honey. It doesn't look good, does it?"

"No, but we'll do our job until the end," Sam said firmly.

Jenny smiled as Sam walked off to where Molly stood huddled with the girls. The woman had been a tremendous help this year. If Jenny was honest with herself, the woman provided a way for Jenny to become a bit lazy, something Jenny would apologize for, and soon.

The buzzer sounded and the crowd cheered as Brandon moved the ball down the court. A few passes later, and the Warriors scored a point. Jenny glanced at the clock and then over at Mark. She wanted them to win so bad it hurt, but not only for the team. Mark had worked so hard with them and she did not want to see him disappointed if they lost.

That last minute sped by quickly, too quickly as a matter of fact. Before she knew it, the final buzzer sounded. The cheers from the crowd turned into groans, and Jenny felt her heart break when she saw the look of disappointment on the boys' faces. She let out a sigh and turned to join the cheer squad.

"Girls," she said as she walked up to the teens, whose faces drooped, "it's been another fun, yet short, season to cheer for our basketball team. I'm so proud of all of you." She made sure she looked into each girl's eyes before continuing. "Progress was made this year by everyone, and I know Coach Molly and I are both pleased."

The girls smiled, though weakly, as people moved around them.

"Are we still going out to grab food?" Mary asked.

"We are. And don't forget to tell the boys how good they did later.

Rest up for the next couple of days; we're going to start volleyball tryouts next week, so if you're interested, it's next Thursday at four."

This made the girls brighten up immensely. They nodded, and after answering a few more questions, Jenny dismissed them.

She looked over hesitantly at Mark and saw he was counseling the players. Unlike those first few weeks, however, he stood tall and proud and held a smile as he gave what Jenny knew were words of encouragement that would take away at least a small portion of the sting losing could leave.

***

Jenny scrubbed at her hair one last time with the towel before wrapping it around her head. By the time they had left the arcade, it had been close to midnight, and she had promised Mark to meet up tomorrow late morning. Grabbing her robe, she slipped it on and then let out a small laugh. She had bought it at a garage sale a few months earlier and simply adored it. It was sea blue with yellow goldfish, and though it was gaudy and a size too big, it was soft, fluffy, and the most comfortable thing she owned. If only she could live in it all day, she'd be happy.

As she headed out of the bathroom and into her bedroom, she went to close the door when she heard a noise behind her. Her heart leapt into her throat and she slowly turned and looked toward the bedroom window. Was someone trying to break in? The curtains were closed, so she was not able to see if anyone was there, but for a moment, all she could do was stand frozen in place, listening closely and waiting for something to happen.

Panic filled her, and she finally came to her senses and ran to grab a softball bat from the closet. This time when the noise sounded again, a light tapping on the window, she shivered as her mind went to a movie she had watched recently where a thief had used some sort of contraption to cut a hole in the window of a house he was breaking into. Why a thief dressed in all black picked her house to rob, she had no idea, but he would pay for it if that was the case.

Summoning all her courage, she tiptoed to the window, her hands wrapped around the bat, which lay poised on her shoulder. Her heart was beating so hard against her chest, she thought it would break through her sternum as she reached for the curtain to draw it back.

"You can do this," she said to herself, glad to at least hear her own voice in the otherwise silent room.

Her hand touched the fabric on the curtain, and she paused to take a deep breath before pulling it back in one quick movement and pulling the bat over her shoulder as if she was waiting for a softball to come flying over home plate.

However, it was not a robber who stood at the window; it was Mark crouched down with a rose in his hand.

"Mark?" she asked incredulously. She shook her head and leaned the bat against the wall. Using both hands, she opened the window and Mark gave her a huge grin. "What are you doing?" she demanded. "You have no idea how bad you scared me!"

The man had no idea how close he came to getting his head bashed in, or at least some part of his body hit.

"I'm sorry. I thought…well, you know, like old times." He thrust the rose forward and Jenny thought her heart would melt.

She took the rose and inhaled its sweet fragrance. "Thank you. This is sweet. What's the occasion?"

"You," he replied as if she should already know that answer. "I thought a woman of your beauty and strength needs to be recognized." Jenny thought she would float up to the sky as he said this. He had always been a romantic at heart. "I hate to be rude, but the climb down doesn't look as easy as it used to. Any chance I can cut through?"

She nodded and then moved aside to let him in. "Sure, but hurry. I don't want Katie getting the wrong idea." She shot him a playful grin.

Katie's voice behind them made Jenny jump. "Honey, with that housecoat on, no one is getting the wrong idea."

This made all three of them laugh, though Jenny could feel her face heat up with embarrassment on so many levels. She helped Mark through the window and then went to close it again.

"Mark's playing Romeo again, huh?" Katie said, still leaning against the door jamb. "What's next? Are you two going to sneak out on your bicycles?"

Jenny narrowed her eyes. "We just might. Is that okay with you?"

Katie shrugged. "Sure. But don't wear that housecoat out in public. That'd be the talk of the town for years." She smiled and turned to head down the hall. "All right, you kids have fun." A moment later, Jenny heard Katie's bedroom door close.

She turned back to Mark. "Come on, let's head downstairs."

When they got to the kitchen, Jenny went to the coffee pot. She could feel Mark's eyes on her as she prepared the coffee and it sent a shiver down her spine. Not that same shiver she had gotten when she thought someone was breaking into her house. No, this time it was a pleasant feeling.

Finally, she could not take it anymore. "Are you staring at me?" she asked without turning.

Mark laughed and then grabbed her hand. She had not even noticed he was standing behind her. "That robe," he said in a mock husky voice, "I mean, I didn't think you dressed so provocatively." This made them both laugh. "I don't know if I can date a girl like that. I might have to get with a more conservative girl…maybe Cindy?"

Jenny gasped as she raised a fist at him. "Don't you even think about it, mister," she warned and then laughed when he pretended to cower. "I mean it. If I see you within a hundred feet of her, you're going to get it!"

Mark laughed and then gently grabbed her fist. "Okay, no more. Please, I don't want to get hurt."

She smiled, but then Mark stepped in closer to her. It seemed as if time stood still as his hands moved to her waist. Through all their dates so far, they had yet to kiss—another step Jenny was delaying as long as possible. Kissing could so easily lead to other emotions she was not ready to feel just yet.

"I never want to hurt you again," he whispered. "I love you, Jenny."

Her heart soared as his lips brushed hers. The kiss was exhilarating and she felt herself melt in his arms. She loved him, there was no denying it.

When the kiss broke, she looked into his eyes, and neither said anything. However, as the silence continued, she could not stop her mind from drudging up that tiny bit of doubt one more time. She knew it was unfair, but she could not bring herself to say the words back to him. Instead, she smiled and grabbed his hands in hers.

"That was beautiful," she said quietly, and she meant it. "Come on, let's get some coffee."

She grabbed two mugs from the cupboard and poured them each a cup. Then she added sugar and creamer to his and handed it to him.

"Perfect," he said after taking a sip.

"Thank you. So, what's next for Coach Mark?"

He walked over to the kitchen table, pulled out a chair and took a seat. Jenny followed, doing the same. "Well," he replied, "that's a good question. Linda wants me to continue with the boys' phys ed classes, of course, but I told her I still have no interest in coaching baseball. I just want to move past it."

Jenny nodded but said nothing.

"I was thinking about maybe talking to Diane in Theater. After telling Dave how I would help him with the Christmas play, I realized that I can still pursue my dream, but at a more local level."

Jenny forced a smile, but her heart was racing. She had thought he had put that all behind him, and now he was going back to pursuing it? What if he caught the acting bug and took off for Hollywood again?

"Are you okay?" Mark asked.

"I'm fine. I'm just tired is all. But keep going."

They stayed up and talked in the kitchen for the next hour, until Mark agreed it was getting late and he needed to get home.

Jenny walked him to the front door and gave him a hug. Though the thought of a quick kiss went through her mind, she did not want to chance it, not in the doorway while she was in a housecoat.

She closed the door after they said goodbye and she returned to the kitchen to clean up. However, she poured herself another cup of coffee instead and went back to sit at the table. F

or years she had hoped Mark would return and they would get back together, and just when she resigned herself that they were done, he showed up to turn her world upside down.

He had gone above and beyond to show her he had changed, and she was madly in love with him again. So, why could she not let go of the past and the fears that came with it?

It was all so confusing, too much to think about at this hour of the night. She turned off the coffee maker and took her mug upstairs with her. After closing the door, she grabbed her Bible and began to read in hopes of finding the Words to guide her.

## *Chapter Twenty*

Thursday evening Mark glanced around at the parents who sat at tables around the library. The PTA meeting was in full swing and excitement was in the air as Linda came to a close on her speech. No parent was here for the information on the bake sale or the new textbooks, they wanted to know about the dance.

When he glanced over at Jenny, he smiled. She sat across the room from him, and as always, no matter what she wore—be it an oversized robe with goldfish on it or the blue blouse and cream-colored slacks she wore now—she looked beautiful.

The previous week, he had told her he loved her, and when they had kissed, he felt that everything in the world was right. However, when the kiss broke, she did not return the sentiment, and it bothered him then as much as it did now. Was it simply her being so caught up in the kiss that she could not find the words?

He let out a small laugh, glad no one looked at him when he did. Did he think he was such a great kisser that it would make a woman speechless and make her lose track of time and space?

No, it was definitely something else. Perhaps he was moving too quickly. That was the only reasonable explanation for her not telling him she loved him back.

"Mark Davis and Jenny Hunter, if you please," Linda said, breaking Mark from his thoughts.

Mark stood and headed over to the podium and smiled as Jenny approached.

"Want me to start?" Jenny whispered. Mark nodded and she approached the small mic on the podium. "It's time again for the annual homecoming dance. As always, we want to provide the students with a fun, yet safe, atmosphere. Now, Mark and I have already worked with the student homecoming committee, and everything looks great and ready to go. But, well, I'll let Mark tell you how you can help."

She took a step back and Mark approached the mic.

"We're in need of chaperons; parents who are willing to come early to help with setup and stay a little after to help with cleanup. We're thinking we could use a few adults to supervise the parking lot throughout the event, and then several parents inside during the dance. So, if there's anyone who'd like to help, please raise your hand." Three men immediately raised their hands. "Perfect. Thank you, gentlemen. If there is anyone else who'd like to help Coach Jenny and me, we'd appreciate it. Remember, this is to assure that everyone at the dance has a good time." Several more hands, perhaps a bit more reluctant but no less appreciated, went up.

Doing a quick head-count, he smiled. "Excellent. Three in the parking lot and seven of us total in the gym. Once again, thank you to everyone who volunteered."

A man stood up. Mark recognized him as Burt Johnson, a middle-aged man who had a tendency to stick his nose in everyone else's business. "How come you're not coaching baseball?" Burt asked. "The team could really use you." He turned to another man who sat nearby, "No offense Bill."

"I appreciate it," Mark replied, "but Bill is doing a great job. My focus is on the phys ed program and possibly theater next semester." Burt snorted as he retook his seat, but he did not say anything in response. Mark glanced over at Jenny, who had an odd frown on her face, but he quickly dismissed it. It probably was directed at Burt.

Linda walked up and placed her hands on the podium as Mark took a step back. "Thank you again for attending this evening. You are dismissed." She wore a proud smile on her face, as if dismissing everyone gave her some sort of power no one else had.

Mark walked over to Jenny. "The dance should be great," he said as she grabbed her purse from the table where she had been sitting. "We have plenty of volunteers now, so it should go without a hitch."

"That's true," Jenny said, "but I'm sure there'll be some sort of drama. There always is." He laughed. She was not wrong there.

They greeted several mutual friends and a short time later headed out to the parking lot. Mark smiled. He had something special planned, something he wanted to ask her.

"So, I need to talk to you about something," he said as they neared her truck.

"Sure. What is it?" She shivered in the chilly wind and Mark took off his blazer and offered it to her. "You're so sweet," she said as she pulled over her shoulders.

"I know I am," he said playfully. He could not help but stare at her; she was simply stunning.

"Well?" she said with an expectant look on her face. "What is it? I can't take the suspense any longer."

He laughed and put his hands in his pockets as he kicked a bit of gravel on the ground. "So, I know you're the most beautiful girl in Hopes Crest," he said, which made her giggle. "And I also know you could pick any guy you wanted." He looked up, making his eyes widen in feigned innocence. "Jenny, would you be my date to the dance?"

Her cheeks reddened and she laughed. "I see," she said, clearly playing along. "I don't know. I have so many choices." She put her hands on her hips and looked him up and down. "You're cute, and I don't usually go out with the sporty type, but yeah, I guess I can do that."

This made them both laugh and then he gave her a quick hug.

"That's great," he said. "I'll wear a suit I bought last year. What're you going to wear?"

She zipped up his blazer and looked down. "Maybe this, or maybe something else." She shrugged. "Either way, it's a surprise."

"Fair enough. So, what do you say we head to yours for some coffee?"

"No way," she said. "If you plan on taking me to the dance, I'm high-maintenance." She walked around the truck and opened the door. "I'll see you at Penny's."

Mark shook his head and laughed as he walked over to his truck. He felt like he was walking on air. Though she had not told him outright that she loved him, he could see it in her eyes. Besides, she was his date for the homecoming dance; nothing could say 'I love you' more than that.

***

Mark leaned forward in his seat at church on Sunday morning. Dave had been preaching for the past twenty minutes on the ten lepers who were healed and how only one came back to thank Jesus, and Mark found himself completely engrossed in the message.

Beside him sat Jenny and next to her Katie. About two hundred people were in attendance and Mark knew many of them; however, there were quite a few new faces dotting the crowd, including many teenagers he knew from the school who sat with their parents. Hopes Crest was growing and yet it still retained its small-town charm, something he was happy about.

"And then," Dave was saying, "this always gets me…'Rise and go; your faith has made you well.' You see, folks, it wasn't because the man was special or that he had brought the pastor a freshly baked apple pie." The congregation chuckled at this because everyone knew Dave loved apple pie. "It was because of faith. Yes, there are times when we feel we have enough faith to fill the world and yet prayers don't get answered. That has many Christians scratching their head. But we'll talk about that next week. Let us close in prayer."

Mark bowed his head, the message hitting home with him. He had a lot to be thankful for, and though it had been tough, he had come to a place in his life where he could be thankful for everything he had.

The prayer ended and then the piano played softly as people began to stand up and leave. Some people stopped to make small talk, but most filed out of the nave, ready to return to whatever it was they did after church. Mark's plans were to go eat with Jenny and Katie at their house.

As they made their way down the aisle with the other parishioners, Dave approached them. "Hey, guys, I'm glad you could make it this week." He gave each of them a quick hug. "Did you manage to stay awake?"

Mark and Jenny both laughed.

"To be honest," Mark said eagerly, "it was a great message. Giving thanks and having faith. And you know, you were right. There are some prayers that go unanswered." Mark was thinking of his failed television pilot. "But others are." He smiled at Jenny, whose cheeks went a bright red.

Dave smiled. "It really makes me happy to hear people receive The Word." He turned to Jenny. "I know it's short notice, but Jenny, is there any chance you could join me and Maria at ours for lunch today?"

She shot Mark a quick glance. "Well, I had plans with Mark, but if you don't mind…"

Mark shook his head. "Not at all. It gives me an excuse to grab a pizza and head home to watch some sports."

Jenny laughed and Dave turned to him. "I'm sure Jenny'll explain it all later, but for now, it's a private meeting, top secret." Dave gave him a wink. "Anyway, Jenny, I'll see you at our place in a few." With that, he walked away.

Mark looked at Jenny. "Have fun and let me know what you find out," he told her as he gave her a quick hug.

"I will. Let's meet up tonight at my house."

Mark nodded and then said goodbye before heading out to the parking lot. It was a great day, and with the thought of pizza on his mind and stomach, he knew things were only going to get better.

***

The aroma of pepperoni and melted cheese was driving Mark insane. He had just picked up his pizza and could not wait to get home and eat. After putting his seatbelt on, he went to drive off but then his phone rang. He did not recognize the number and almost canceled the call but decided at the last minute to take it anyway.

"Hello?" he asked, his voice hesitant.

A familiar voice replied on the other end of the line. "Mark? Is that you? It's me, Karen." Mark's eyes went wide, his heart racing. Karen was his agent, and he hadn't spoken to her since he moved back to Hope.

"Yeah, it's me," he said. "How are you?" He tried to wrack his brain as to why she would be calling him. He was sure he had made it pretty clear he was finished with Hollywood when he left.

"I'm well," she replied. "You're not going to believe this, but Movieflix has been looking at picking up a new series title, and they've been in some serious talks about the pilot you did over the summer. Don't you see, Mark? You're going to costar in a series!" She let out an ecstatic laugh.

Mark's heart and mind went in a thousand different directions. He was excited beyond belief. After putting in all that hard work, all those auditions, all that time, his dream was finally going to come true.

Yet, he was in Hopes Crest trying to rebuild a life he had wanted forever, and the two outcomes warred against each other in his head; so much so that he sat there in complete silence without saying a word.

"Mark, are you there?"

He shook his head to clear his mind. "Yes, sorry. Wow, that's amazing. When're they going to start filming? And what about pay? Have they made an offer yet?"

"I don't know many specific details yet, but I can assure you it will be above scale. They're going to want you in by…let me see…" Mark heard the shuffling of papers in the background, "November ninth. Yep, that's it. Come in on the ninth to meet with them, and you should be shooting within a week. Congratulations."

Mark nodded, even though she could not see him, as he tried to work moisture back into his mouth. "Yeah, that's great. Karen, is there any chance I can call you back later? This has hit me out of the blue and I need some time to process it."

"Of course, absolutely," she replied. "Just make sure you get back to me as soon as possible. They'll need an answer right away."

“Okay, no problem,” Mark replied and a minute later he hung up and started driving toward home. Was this opportunity like the message today about faith? Had his faith paid off and the result was just delayed longer than he had expected?

His eyes scanned the shops in Hopes Crest as he drove past. Was he truly destined to leave again? He wasn't sure, but his heart went to Jenny. Would she be willing to walk away and come with him to follow his dream this time?

It was too all too overwhelming to think about at the moment. What he needed right now was to keep his mind busy before he could sit down and truly make a decision, and the large pizza beside him would help him do just that.

## *Chapter Twenty-One*

Jenny headed out to the parking lot at church. She wondered what Pastor Dave and Maria wanted to talk to her about. The wind was blowing steadily, and for once she was glad she had remembered to bring the coat she pulled in tighter around her.

The parking lot was emptying quickly, and she turned when she heard someone call out her name.

"Hey, Coach Jenny," Sam said, walking up to her.

Jenny smiled and gave the girl a hug. "Hi, Sam. How are you?"

"Good. I'm excited about volleyball this week," she said, and Jenny smiled. "I'm set and I know Emma and a few other girls are ready to try out."

"Well, I look forward to seeing you all there," Jenny said. Then Sam bit at her lip. Jenny recognized when a person wanted to say something, especially one of her team members, and Sam had all the signs. "What's going on, sweetie? Is something on your mind?"

Sam let out a deep breath. "It's Kyle," she said, shaking her head. "The dance is just a few weeks away and he hasn't asked me yet. It's kind of got me worried."

Jenny smiled. "You have to realize that boys…well, sometimes they're forgetful," she said, which made Sam laugh. "It might be that he's forgotten or maybe he's waiting for the right time to ask you. He seems like a gentleman, after all."

Sam seemed to consider this. "He is a nice guy, but he drives me crazy sometimes. I still like him, though."

Jenny laughed and glanced over as Kayla got into her truck. She noticed James, Kayla's boyfriend, who walked over to his truck, as well.

"What does your mom think?" she asked, turning her attention back to Sam.

"I didn't ask her first. I thought I would ask you."

This surprised Jenny. "Oh? Why's that?"

"Well, you're Coach Jenny," Sam explained as if Jenny should already know this. "You're young and pretty and all the girls like you and look up to you."

The compliments made Jenny's heart soar. She complained at times about working with the girls, but in all reality, she loved it. They were great to be around and she was honored they felt they could confide in her. "You're too sweet," she said, giving Sam another hug. "Hey, how're you getting home? Your mom and James just left; do you need a ride?"

Sam shook her head. "No. I'm going with Kyle and his parents to lunch. Oh, here they are. I'll talk to you later." She hurried off to a blue sedan Jenny recognized as belonging to the Rogers family, Kyle standing outside the passenger side back door.

Jenny smiled as she headed over to her truck. Once she was in, she started it and tapped her fingers on the steering wheel. It had been almost a week since Mark had told her he loved her, and though the words had been beautiful, she still struggled with how to proceed. She watched as Sam slid into the back seat of Kyle's parents' car and Kyle closed the door before walking around to the other side, and her smile widened. Kyle was a kind young man who would grow into a mature adult, there was no doubt about it. She had never heard of him being in any kind of trouble, besides a few groundings his parents had given him, and she had never seen anything to say he was anything but the gentleman Sam saw him as.

As Jenny put the truck into drive, her mind returned to Mark. He had opened the door for her on many occasions, climbed her roof, and even made a picnic lunch for her on home plate. But most importantly, he had shown how sorry he was for what he had done all those years ago. He had proven he loved her in more ways than words could have, and she bit at her lip. It was about time she told him how she felt, as well.

***

Jenny pulled up to Pastor Dave's house and parked on the street. She recognized Kayla's truck in the driveway, and the truck door opened and Kayla stepped out.

"Hey, you," Kayla said, giving her a quick hug. "I'm so excited."

Jenny stepped back, confused. "What do you mean? Do you know what this is about?"

Kayla grabbed her hands, glanced toward the door and then looked back at Jenny. "I don't know for sure, but I talked to Dave about the teen girls' group last week. I'm thinking that that's why he wants to meet with us."

"That's awesome. You know, even just today, Sam..." Jenny said, then let her words trail off. She didn't mean to throw Sam under the bus like that.

"Let me guess," Kayla replied, "she asked you for advice?" Jenny nodded and Kayla smiled. "It's okay. We share a lot, definitely more than we did six months ago, but girls need a confidante, and I'm honored she went to you."

"Oh stop. I'm going to cry," Jenny said, feeling all fuzzy inside.

"And I'm hungry," Dave said from behind them, making both of them jump. "You ladies, come on."

They followed him up the driveway and through the front door. Maria was just putting a pan in the oven when they walked into the kitchen, her jet-black hair pulled back into a ponytail. Jenny had always thought she was very pretty with her olive skin and high cheekbones.

"Hey, girls," Maria said as she walked over to them and pulled them each into a hug. "I'm so glad you came. And I bet you're wanting to know what's going on." Jenny and Kayla both nodded as Maria turned to Dave, who was helping himself to a breadstick. "Dave, that's for the lasagna. Now, put it down and talk to these women."

"Yes, dear," he said and then rolled his eyes, which earned him a playful punch in the arm. "OK, I'll stop. Let's head into the living room. We have some time, right?"

"Forty minutes," Maria said and they made their way down a short hallway. The three women sat on the couch as Dave went to a recliner.

"So, Kayla approached me about you two running a girls' meeting once a month or something," Dave said and Jenny nodded. "The truth is, Maria and I've been talking about that for a while now. We've noticed that the church congregation is growing, and more teens are joining. Now, both of you are respected members, not only in the church, but in the community…"

Maria cut him off. "Dave, get to the point," she said in exasperation. "The suspense is killing them."

Dave sat up and let out a sigh. "Fine. We're going to start expanding to a Wednesday night service come the New Year. The teens need their own service that deals with the issues facing them today. What I'm asking is would you be interested in teaching on Wednesday nights? Basically, I'd like to know if you'd both be our teen outreach leaders."

Jenny smiled. The idea was more than appealing to her, and Wednesdays fit her schedule perfectly. Plus, she loved the kids, and when she turned to Kayla, she saw that the woman was just as excited as she was.

"I'd love to," Jenny said and Kayla echoed the same.

Maria smiled at them, gave them a single nod, and then headed into the kitchen as if they had answered exactly as she had expected.

Dave continued. "Great." Then he turned to Kayla. "I was thinking that maybe James might be interested in helping, with a boys' group, of course. What do you think?"

Kayla nodded. "I know he would." She answered with complete certainty.

"Of course, I'm going to ask Mark," he said to Jenny. "My thinking is to take the first and third Wednesdays of each month and have separate meetings to focus on issues each group deals with.

Then the other Wednesdays you can have co-ed services. We could also start talking about summer camps and making plans to begin next summer. We'll need leaders for those, too, and I'd love to have you both on board to help run them. How does that sound?"

Jenny could not think of anything else that she would want to do more than minister to the teenagers in the area, and she agreed and Kayla agreed just as quickly. Everything was coming together; Mark was back in her life, she had a job she loved, and she now had a way to help the next generation. With a wonderful future falling into place, she could not think of a better time to finally express to Mark how she felt about him and tell him that she loved him.

## *Chapter Twenty-Two*

The Town Square was relatively empty and most of the businesses in the area were closed for the evening as Jenny pulled her truck into an empty parking space. She had called Mark earlier and asked him to meet her in the park so she could share her exciting news with him, and he had come right back at her that he had news to share with her, too. Jenny saw this as a good sign.

As Jenny got out of her truck, a police cruiser slowed down and came to a stop behind her. Joanna Lawrence, Jo to most who knew her, was a thirty-something local and also the sheriff of Hopes Crest.

"Hey there, Jenny," the sheriff said after rolling down the passenger window of the cruiser. "How are you?"

Jenny leaned against the car door and looked through the window. "Doing good. How about yourself?"

Jo looked around the Town Square. "Oh, you know, same problems day in and day out. High crime, fights, stabbings." Jo always did have a good sense of humor.

Jenny caught sight of Mark pulling his truck into a space on the other side of the square. Jo must have, as well, because she said, "I'd better let you go or Mark's going to go crazy waiting for you."

"How'd you know we were together?" Jenny asked suspiciously.

The sheriff snorted. "It's Hopes Crest. We know everyone's business."

Jenny laughed as Jo pulled away. The cruiser made the lap around the Square and gave a short honk at Mark, who responded with a quick wave. Jenny jogged across the street and through the small park, joy carrying her steps as she ran up to Mark and threw her arms around him.

"You have no idea the kind of news I have," she said as she tried to catch her breath. "I've been dying to tell you all day! It's beyond…awesome!"

She felt like a million bucks as he took her hands in his and smiled widely. "I have good news, too, but I want you to go first."

She nodded. "Okay. So, long story short, Dave's going to start a Wednesday night group right after the New Year, and he wants Kayla and me to run it! Isn't that great?" She gave him another hug of excitement. "But that's not all. He wants you and James to help, too, with the boys. That way, twice a month, the boys and girls can go out and do something in their own groups or have studies at the church; whatever we decide and then other Wednesdays we'll all work together and do mixed Bible studies and deal with current teenage issues. He's even talking about the possibility of creating summer camps. Is that not cool or what?"

She was out of breath by the time she finished. "Sorry, I talk too much. But, Mark, I've been thinking. We've had our ups and downs, but this is another way God has put us together." The excitement she felt was almost overwhelming. "And I should've told you this last week…"

The wind picked up as she stepped in closer to him and her arms went around his neck. His face was so handsome, his heart and soul kind, and she could not imagine being apart from him ever again. "I love you. If I look back, I find that I never stopped loving you."

His hand moved to her cheek and he wiped away a tear. "Jenny, you have no idea how much I love you," he whispered, his eyes gleaming. "I thought about you every single moment I was gone, and that's why I want you to head out to California with me."

She pulled away from him. "California?" she asked in confusion. Had he not heard a single word she had just said? How did moving to California play into those plans?

"Yes!" he said with great enthusiasm. "Karen, my agent, called me earlier and Movieflix has picked up the pilot I shot. They're going to film a whole season!" He grabbed her hands and squeezed them. "Don't you see? My dream's come true!"

Jenny's heart dropped as she took in his wide smile. He really had not heard what she had said. And worse, it was like a bad dream. No, it was more than that; it was a nightmare from the past repeating itself in the present. A bolt of anger formed in her stomach as Mark continued to talk, his enthusiasm never waning.

"Last time I was a fool trying to hurry us into getting married and asking you to take a chance on the unknown. But this time I have guaranteed money. Even if I get scale, and I get to shoot over twenty-plus episodes, I'm going to have some major money coming in by the time we're done. And if the first season takes off, then there is a good chance at adding more seasons, which will mean even better money. Just think! I might end up with my own star on the Walk of Fame!"

"Mark, I…" she started to say, but her heart and mind were racing every which way and she was much too stunned to even comprehend how she felt beyond a fog of confusion.

"Just listen for a moment, please," he said. Jenny found herself nodding silently, not because she wanted to hear what he had to say but because she was too stunned to speak. "I fly out the ninth of next month. I'll get us each an apartment until we get married, and only if you want to get married. You can work if you want or just relax by the pool; whatever you want. I'll be able to take care of you now."

"The ninth?" Jenny gasped. "That's the night of the homecoming dance." Tears filled her eyes. Was fate meant to torment her twice in the same setting? "What about the theater group at school? Or the one at church? Mark, Dave wants you as a leader here."

Mark nodded as if he had already considered this. "Just think how much more helpful it'll be if I'm famous," he reasoned. "We can come back a few times a year, at least, and help everyone, and you can visit Katie and anyone else you want. Shoot, have her move out there, too! I'll pay for everything." He gave her a pleading look. "What do you say? Are you ready this time?"

A car pulled up a few spaces down and a family of four got out and she watched them laugh with each other. She looked around the Town Square. The shops, the people, the memories. Hopes Crest was her home, not some apartment in Hollywood.

"Mark," she said as she looked down at the ground, "I don't know. It's a lot to think about." Inside, her mind screamed 'No! Why should I give up everything?'

"That's understandable," he replied. "I want you to think about it, and I think you'll see that it's going to be worth it."

"I take it that, if I decide not to leave, you're going to go anyway?"

He nodded as he turned around and stared over at the park. "Hopes Crest will always be home to me, but you know I've always wanted to be an actor. I gave up on that dream, but the dream didn't give up on me." He turned back to her. "I want you to be a part of that dream."

Jenny felt her anger finally rise through the fog of confusion. All of her worst fears had come true. Each step along the way led to this point over the last few months, and warning bells had gone off in her head, fear that he would take off again one day. She had ignored it all, but now the day she had feared had arrived. To make matters worse, she had just confessed her love to him after guarding her heart for so long. How he managed to accept it and then still decide he wanted to go away was beyond her.

"I'll think it over," she said, though she already knew what her answer would be. "I mean, you're giving me just over a week to decide, and that's a lot of pressure."

"That's fine," he replied. He did not seem too worried, and that pulled at her heart, but right now she needed to focus on what would be best for her. "Do you want to grab a coffee?" he asked.

"I can't," she said, the words sounding strangled as she looked down at the ground. She cleared her throat. "I told Katie I'd spend some time with her." She did not like the fact she had just lied to him, but how did he expect her to think about her future at the drop of a hat, especially if she was constantly reminded of what he wanted her to do?

He pulled her in for a hug, and she tried to not make it too stiff. "Think about it and let me know soon. I have a lot of plans to make." Then he added in a whisper in her ear, "I love you."

"Love you," she said in a choked reply.

The hug broke and then a few moments later Jenny was heading back to her truck. Her stomach hurt, her jaw was tight with anger and resentment, and her step no longer was light.

As she headed home, she wondered if she was meant to remain single because obviously relationships were not her thing. Everything had fallen apart before, and now it was happening all over again.

***

The sun had gone down completely as Jenny sat with Katie in the living room, each with a cup of coffee in her hand. Jenny had just finished telling Katie about her meeting with Mark, ending with her telling him she would think about whether or not she would go with him to California.

Rather than backing her up as Jenny had expected, Katie instead said, "I think you should really think about it, Jenny. Think and pray about it."

"I said I would," Jenny replied moodily. Katie had been the one person Jenny felt she could count on to be on her side. However, it seemed even Katie was not going to take sides this time. Somehow Jenny felt betrayed, though that was unfair of her to say. Katie had always been a wonderful friend, and in all honesty, she would never let Jenny down. She never had, and she never would.

"I mean it," Katie said as she stood. "Give it some good thought before you go spouting off an answer based only on emotion."

"Fine," Jenny said reluctantly.

"All right, I'm heading to bed." Katie leaned down and gave Jenny a hug. "Don't forget, pray and think."

"Yeah, yeah," Jenny mumbled in reluctant reply.

When Katie was gone, Jenny went to the kitchen and rinsed their mugs and placed them in the dishwasher. Then she followed Katie's example and headed to her bedroom.

However, rather than getting ready for bed, Jenny went instead to her closet and pulled out the blue prom dress she had kept all these years.

Tears streamed down her face as her hand moved across the silky material. The dress had been the surprise she had promised Mark for the homecoming dance, and it would have been fun to chaperon in it—and maybe even sneak in a dance with him. But now that dream was gone. It was obvious Mark cared nothing for her feelings as he painted his picture of the wonderful life in California he promised they would have.

The metal hanger clicked loudly on the metal rod as she hung the dress back in her closet. Then something caught her eye. She pulled out a photo album from a shelf and carried it to the bed. Lying on her stomach, she flipped through the pages and allowed her mind to wander into the past.

She revisited the games, the parties, and those precious moments she and Mark had spent together, all in and around Hopes Crest. This town was where her heart resided and she could not picture herself living anywhere else.

"Well, Jenny, you did again," she whispered as she turned the page. "You fell for the guy and let him stomp on your heart."

She scolded herself for being allowed to be charmed by his words once again. Even as she looked at the happy faces that stared back at her from the many photos in the album, she knew that Mark had always been selfish, always thinking about what he wanted and not about what they would want together. He had not changed one bit.

Closing the photo album, she walked over and placed it back on the shelf in the closet. As she closed the closet door, an old saying went through her mind.

'Fool me once, shame on you. Fool me twice, shame on me.'

"Yes, shame on me," she said as she got into bed. She turned off the lights and pulled the covers over her. "Shame on me, indeed."

## *Chapter Twenty-Three*

Mark felt as if his feet were dancing on air. In the blink of an eye, everything he had ever wished for, every dream he had ever had, was about to come true. Now he just needed to talk to the school principal. He was not proud to be giving her such short notice, but he believed she would understand.

So, he gave Carol a quick wave as he entered the main office. Carol waved back absently, never really taking her attention from her phone call as she nodded toward the hallway that led to Linda's office.

He whispered a quick 'thanks' and headed down the hall and tapped a knuckle on the open door.

"Oh, Mark, come on in," Linda said from behind her desk. "Please, shut the door."

"Hi, Linda," he said as he did as she asked and shut the door behind him.

She pointed to the chair in front of her desk and smiled. "Is everything okay? You seemed a bit excited on the phone."

He gave her a wide smile as he took a seat. He had already let Pastor Dave know his intentions yesterday, and now he hoped this would go as smoothly. "Everything's great," Mark replied. "Never better."

He could not stop the smile from growing as he waited for her to remove her glasses and let them hang on the silver chain around her neck.

"I am very pleased to hear that," she replied. "So, what can I help you with?"

He scooted forward in the chair. "Well, I have some great news. A few days ago, my agent Karen called me."

He gave her a brief rundown on what had transpired. Though he was not looking for permission to leave—that had already been settled; he was leaving regardless of whether he had permission from her or not—he did want to leave on good terms.

When he finished, she leaned back in her chair. "I see," she said. "I can have Bill take over the afternoon phys ed class, I suppose." She sounded as if there was a problem with no solution, even though she did have one.

Mark had already devised a plan in case there was any resistance. "You know, I was thinking. Would it be okay if I asked them to use your name in one of episodes?" he asked. "You've been such an important part of my life, I figure that if they ever do an episode that takes place in a school, the principal's name can be Linda Miller. It's the least I can do as a way to thank you for everything you've done for me."

It was not a lie but a stretched truth; however, if the opportunity did arise, he would ask if they could. It did not mean they would take the suggestion.

This made her smile, just as he suspected it would. "Make sure they hire some young, good-looking woman, of course, with a flattering figure like I have."

"I wouldn't have it any other way," he replied firmly. He suspected she was imagining herself being portrayed by some version of Ingrid Bergman or Julia Roberts.

"Well, young man," she said finally, "you have my blessing. When will be your last day?"

"Friday the eighth," he replied as he pulled himself from the chair after she stood up from hers.

She had a shocked look on her face. "So soon? That's too bad; you won't be able to chaperon the dance."

He reached out to open the door and a pang of guilt ran through him. He had not really thought about the dance, though he recalled only slightly that Jenny might have said something concerning it yesterday.

He had been so excited to share his news he had not been paying that much attention.

"Well, it's in good hands," he said, knowing everything would be fine with one less chaperon. "Thank you again, Linda, for everything."

She smiled and gave him a small hug. "Just remember to stop by and see me when you come back to visit."

"You know I will," he said and then headed out.

With that out of the way, he needed to talk to Jenny. He knew she had a big decision to make, and giving her time to think about it last night rather than demanding her answer right away had been the right thing to do. He had made that mistake last time, and he did not want a repeat of their past performance.

Now, however, he was excited to hear her answer. She had said she loved him, so he was more than confident what her answer would be.

As he walked through the school hallways to the gym, a thought suddenly occurred to him. What if she did not want to go? However, after several moments, he laughed.

They were no longer in high school; they were adults, and one way or another she would be coming. He was almost certain of it. When he opened the door to the office, he smiled when he saw her working at her desk.

"Good afternoon, Coach," he said cheerfully.

She looked up and smiled. "Hey," she replied.

He walked up and pulled his chair in front of her desk. She had gone back to writing, flipping through notebooks, and he sat down and was soon tapping his foot on the floor.

"Mark, you're tapping again," she said in an irritated voice.

"Sorry."

She went back to writing, and he found himself simply staring at her. She was so beautiful, and it occurred to him he could easily get her a walk-on role on the show. Maybe he could get her a real audition. She would make a perfect TV or movie star.

"Do you plan to stare at me all day?" she asked, bringing him back to reality.

"Sorry. So, about yesterday. Did you think about California?" He could feel the knots in his stomach tighten as she methodically set her pen down and closed the notebook.

"It's been roughly twenty-four hours," she said. "So, no, I don't know at this point, okay?" She was clearly growing angry, and he regretted mentioning it.

He hoped she knew how excited he was for them and the possibilities ahead. Then a thought came to mind. There was a way to show her. "Hey, listen, do you have any free nights this week?"

She shook her head and leaned back in her chair. "I have practice all week. Then the girls have a volleyball scrimmage with Silver Ridge on Thursday, and Friday night Molly and I are taking the team out for pizza."

Mark pursed his lips in thought. "Okay, what about Saturday at my place?"

She appeared to think. "We have a practice game here at two, but after that I'm free."

"Perfect," he said as he stood up. "Meet me at my place at six. You're going to love what I have planned. It's a surprise, but I can…"

"We're at work," she cut in pointedly before he could finish his sentence. "We have to keep this professional, remember?"

Her words did not diminish his enthusiasm. "You're right." He pulled the chair back to his desk and he thought back to the tiny student desk he had been forced to use when he first started in August. His desk was still smaller than Jenny's, but at least he fit under it with an adult-sized chair.

He shot Jenny a quick glance. She needed space, that much was clear, and he was going to give it to her. His mind turned to his plans for Saturday as he stared down at his planner. He would have the most perfect date set up, and by the end of the night, she would be more excited than he was about making this move, of that he was certain.

***

The rest of the week flew by, and Mark had been so busy, he had spent very little time outside of work with Jenny. Between volleyball practices and his busy schedule, including his addiction meeting at the library which fell during this week, he had missed her dearly.

They had gone to Penny's for a quick cup of coffee, but they had not had time to really talk about the move. Plus, he did not want to spoil his intricate plan for Saturday night.

Now he paced the living room at his house as he waited for her to come by. Luckily, his parents were out of town for the weekend, so he had the place to himself. For now.

He glanced around the living room, happy with what he saw. He had borrowed two of his mother's easels, covered them with white sheets, and between them sat the coffee table, also covered with a sheet, tiny lumps poking up underneath it.

Everything was in place, and he could not wait for her surprised expression when revealed what he had spent hours planning for her.

He glanced at the clock. It was ten past six; Jenny was late, and Mark found himself questioning whether or not she would even show up. However, when the doorbell finally rang, he hurried to the door to find Jenny standing there, her arms clasped in front of her.

"Hey, you," he said as he closed the door behind them and pulled her in for a hug. She hugged him back, but something was missing from it. However, he dismissed it as nervousness as he stepped back and smiled at her.

"Sorry I'm late," she said. "I got caught up talking with Kayla."

"It's okay. Hey, can I take your coat?" She shook her head no, which he found odd, but rather than dwell on it, he led her to the living room. "Please, have a seat. Would you like something to drink? Coffee? Tea? Water?"

"No, thank you," she said as she glanced at the sheet-covered easels. She still had her hands clasped in front of her, and Mark figured she was probably as nervous as he was, so rather than bugging her about it, he decided to ignore it.

"Okay, so we can grab some food in a bit, but let me show you what I did." He walked over to the coffee table. "Do you remember how we used to watch *The Price is Right* together?" When she nodded, he continued. "Well, this is like the Show Case at the end. I know it's corny, but check it out."

When she said nothing, he swallowed hard and then whipped the sheet off the coffee table in a theatrical manner. On the table sat a toy car, a log cabin he had constructed from Popsicle sticks when he was a kid, and a few other items.

"Your prize package starts off with both of us taking an exciting road trip," he announced as he squatted down and moved the car across the table. "We will take our time exploring the back roads of America, experiencing the worst roadside eateries and cheap motels along the way." He glanced over, expecting a smile or even a laugh. However, when he saw or heard neither, he continued with his demonstration.

"On day three, we will stop for one night in the fabulously exciting city of Las Vegas. Not only will we enjoy one of the fine shows along the Strip, but we will also stuff our faces at one of their famous buffets. But don't worry, we are going to skip the wedding chapels." He laughed at his own joke and moved the car to the front of the log cabin.

"Once we arrive at our new apartments," he then moved to the first easel and removed the sheet, "you will spend a wonderful day shopping on Rodeo Drive. But don't spend too much, at least for the time being." He chuckled at his joke but then bit his lip when he realized she had remained silent.

Trying to remain unperturbed, he moved over to the second easel, but before he could remove the sheet, her voice stopped him.

"Mark, enough. We need to talk."

## *Chapter Twenty-Four*

Jenny shook her head at Mark's attempt to convince her to go to Hollywood with him. Though he had put a lot of effort into it, it didn't matter; she had made up her mind.

"Mark, enough. We need to talk."

He nodded and placed his hands into the front pockets of his jeans. "Okay, we can skip Las Vegas if you want. I've always wanted to try a slot machine, though. Maybe I could run in while you wait in the car." When Jenny still did not comment about Las Vegas, he quickly added, "Fine, we don't even have to go there. I don't care all that much about Las Vegas anyway."

Jenny stood up, her heart heavy, her legs weak. "Mark, I'm not going." She hated seeing the pain in his eyes and the hurt look on his face, but she had made up her mind and it was time to tell him how she felt. "I thought it over, and I can't go."

"I don't understand," he said, confusion on his face. "I thought you loved me."

"I do love you, Mark, and I think I always will to a degree. But we're two different people now, and this is not who I am." She indicated the display as she said the last part.

He shook his head. "No," he demanded. "That's not right at all. We have so much in common. I mean, from the church to the school, our friends, we're connected in so many ways."

"That's right, we are. But they're all here, Mark. Not in Hollywood, but here in Hopes Crest."

He held up a hand. "OK. I get I," he said, though doubt filled his words. "It was way too early for you to decide, and I needed to give you more time.

I see that now. So, how about this? I'll head out there first and then, come Christmas, I can fly back and visit. We'll still see each other until you're ready to move out for good."

Jenny groaned. He was not getting it, and though it would not be easy, there was only one way to make him understand. With the past playing out in front of her again, it was her time to make the decision, not his. "Mark, it's over between us," she said firmly, though inside she was breaking into a million pieces. "I'm sorry, but we're through."

She wiped at her eyes when she saw the pain etched on his face. She did not want to hurt him, but it seemed to be the only way to get him to see the truth. They were either a couple here in Hopes Crest, or they were not a couple at all.

"Jenny, don't say that. Why would you want to do that, after all we've been through?"

Jenny felt her anger finally break the surface. "Are you serious?" She tried not to scream the words, but she could not stop the sting in her tone. "You walked out on me four years ago, left me with a broken heart, and now you're doing it all over again."

"But I'm not leaving you. I want you to go with me. I don't even care when you come to join me, but join me eventually."

"No, it doesn't work like that. You don't come back into town sweet-talking me, make me fall in love again, and then start planting roots, all on the pretext of us starting a life together here. That's what you did. You rekindled your life here and that's the reason I decided to date you again. It's the reason I fell in love with you again, but now, I regret that I did." She held back tears as Mark walked toward her. "No," she said, raising her hand to stop his advance. She was afraid to be held by him; her anger could so easily turn to something else, and right now the anger was the life vest that kept her from drowning.

"This has always been my dream; you know that." His voice was quiet.

"I did know that. It was a dream you said was over. Again, I agreed to date you because your promised you were not going anywhere. Now, you're doing it all over again." She headed to the door.

"It's over Mark. We're done."

He called out to her as she opened the front door and headed out into the night, but she refused to stop, refused to have him see her crying yet again.

Loud footsteps came up behind her and his hand came to her shoulder. "Jenny," he said, his voice choked. She stopped and closed her eyes. Then she turned and her heart broke again when he saw tears matching her own rolling down his cheeks. "I love you. No matter what, I still love you and will never stop loving you. Maybe at work, next week…"

"I told Linda I have a family emergency and won't be at work," she said in a forced calm. "Please, don't call me or talk to me ever again. Goodbye, Mark." She turned and moved quickly to the truck, the teardrops falling faster than her feet moved.

After slamming the door, she started up the truck and pulled out of the drive. She glanced over and saw Mark standing under the porch light, which highlighted his face. It was a handsome face, but the pain and hurt on it made her feel sick.

However, they needed to make a clean break because he had once again made a decision based on his needs without any consideration of hers.

***

Pastor Dave stood before the pulpit before the congregation on Sunday morning, but Jenny found it difficult to pay attention. Katie had left the day before to go to Denver to visit family and so, when Jenny had broken up with Mark—for the second time—she had gone home to an empty house and her own thoughts to haunt her all night.

How could the pain be as strong as it had been the first time? Shouldn't everything be easier the second time around?

Yet, here she sat, alone, the anguish still as fresh as it had been on prom night four years earlier. Not even a night left alone crying had helped.

The decision to not leave with Mark had not been an easy one. However, her life was here in Hopes Crest; she knew this was where God wanted her to be. So many doors had opened at the school and at church, so many opportunities that led to her realizing her dreams. Whenever she tried to picture herself in some apartment over a thousand miles away, she saw nothing but an empty life.

Mark sat next to Dolores in the front row. She had to admit he looked handsome in his suit, but she could not allow herself to be pulled away from her decision simply because she thought he looked good. There was more to a relationship than looks, after all.

She pulled her attention back to the sermon with a sigh. She was here to learn, not to moon over Mark.

"I want to read over this scripture from First Corinthians chapter thirteen one more time," Dave was saying, "and ask you all to think about the importance of its words." Jenny looked down at her open Bible and read the text as Dave read it aloud.

> Love suffers long and is kind; love does not envy; love does not parade itself, is not puffed up; does not behave rudely, does not seek its own, is not provoked, thinks no evil; does not rejoice in iniquity, but rejoices in the truth; bears all things, believes all things, hopes all things, endures all things.

Dave continued reading, but something tugged at Jenny's heart, something she struggled to comprehend. God wanted to tell her something, but she seemed at a loss as to what that was.

"But here, this part," Dave continued, "is my favorite part. If you think of anything this week, think of the following from verse thirteen. 'And now abide faith, hope, love, these three; but the greatest of these is love.'" He removed the mic from the podium and walked to the top of the steps. Jenny felt as if he were looking right at her when he spoke again.

"God is love. It is the reason Jesus died for our sins. You see, we can have faith in things, hope in things to come, but without love, it is all futile. Love is never easy. As a matter of fact, a lot of times it's hard.

It's hard loving those who disagree with you. Or those who cause you pain. But in all things we have to love each other."

Jenny stared at him as if transfixed. She could not stop the warm feeling that spread through her body as Dave spoke.

"So, this week, I would ask that you do that. Love the person who doesn't love you back. Love the coworker who got the promotion instead of you. And if you're not sure if you should show love, ask yourself this: 'Are my actions showing love, or something opposite?' Anger, jealousy, pride, selfishness, those are just examples of many opposites of love." He returned to the podium and replaced the mic.

"Before we close in prayer, I would like Mark Davis to stand up."

Jenny looked across the aisle as Mark stood and her heart beat against her chest.

"Mark has been given an opportunity to return to Hollywood and maybe become famous," Dave said, and people began to speak to one another in hushed tones. "Make sure you wish him the best. Now, let's close in prayer."

Jenny bowed her head as Dave began to pray. Though her heart hurt, her own prayer was simple.

"Help me understand what love is."

## *Chapter Twenty-Five*

The air cooled significantly over the next week, and Mark had not seen Jenny during that time. The trees now stood devoid of leaves, and a light but cold breeze rustled up what had not already been raked up by home and business owners. Those that had flown into the street crunched under the tires of Mark's truck as he pulled into the school parking lot, which sat empty since it was Saturday morning. He had to be at the airport by mid-afternoon, but he felt the need to stop and see the baseball diamond one last time before he left.

Karen had called earlier to confirm that he was indeed coming and she had agreed to meet him at LAX at six to pick him up. At least he would not have to pay for a taxi, which was nice. Tomorrow, he would be at the corporate office of Movieflix, where he would be presented a contract and then start his new career.

He was finally realizing his dream, after all these years. Though he should feel ecstatic, however, he found that he felt far from it. Fate had a strange way of rearing its ugly head, and he had once again managed to screw things up.

He opened the door, stepped out into the cool air, and pulled his coat tighter around him. The night he told Jenny his good news replayed in his head as he stared out at the field.

Her lack of excitement and her changed demeanor should have been a clear sign. However, he had ignored her initial reaction, or rather his eagerness to have her go with him had overshadowed his ability to read her.

What he should have done was taken it slow rather than piling everything on her at once. It was too late for that now, though. Now it was over.

The realization that there was no more Mark and Jenny haunted him, and it left him with a nauseated feeling. Why was it when one dream became a reality, the other was taken from him?

He had been steadfast in prayer, and it seemed God had opened the door for him in Hollywood, but now, as that door opened, the one with Jenny had closed. It was as if he was supposed to have only one dream and not both, and it left an empty feeling inside him.

He smiled as he looked up at the Hopes Crest High School building. The place held so many wonderful memories, and he would miss the staff and the kids he had worked with.

They had made such wonderful progress throughout the season, and he could not help but feel an overwhelming pride for them. Maybe next year they would make it even further with a new coach, but he had to admit that the thought of someone else coaching instead of him made him sad.

The baseball field looked barren in the weak late fall sun. As much as he had hated the sport, somehow he was always drawn back to this field, and he was not sure why. Gone was the green grass of the outfield, now replaced by the brown of impending winter. Though he would be back for Christmas, he wanted to get in one more lap around the bases, so, heading to the batter's box, he replayed the events from the state championship in his head, just as he had so many times before. Then he threw down his imaginary bat and began his jog around the bases, but this time as he came around third, no one would be there, no teammates, no Jenny, no one to greet him. No, only he was there…alone.

As his foot touched home, the truth hit him harder than it ever had before. No one was there. He was alone now, and there was nothing he could do about it. The thought sent a shiver down his spine and he looked up at the gray sky. It held a promise of snow, but he would be high in the air by the time it began to fall.

He took one last look around the field and shook his head. Dreams started and ended here for many aspiring ballplayers, but he had been the only one who really had a chance. However, he did not care about that because he would soon realize his true dream.

He walked back to the truck but stopped when a car pulled up. He smiled when he saw Kyle get out of the car. It was nice to see at least one of his players before he left; he had not thought much about how he would miss the students, or at least he tried not to think about it.

"Hey, Coach," Kyle called out. "I was heading into town and saw your truck parked here. Are you on your way to the airport?"

"I sure am." Just saying the words gave Mark a mixture of emotions.

"Well, we're going to miss you. If you come back to visit, will you say hi to us?" The innocence and kindness of Kyle's voice sent a bolt of guilt through Mark's heart. Like most of the teens in the school, he was a good kid.

"I will," Mark replied.

"Okay, good," Kyle said with a wide smile. He kicked at the dirt with the toe of his shoe and had a goofy smile on his face. "It's the big dance tonight. I'm excited for it, but I forgot to buy Sam a corsage." He screwed up his face in confusion and looked up at Mark. "Do they really like that kind of stuff?"

Mark laughed, remembering the corsage he had bought for Jenny all those years ago. "Oh, yeah, trust me, you'll want to be sure you get her one or you'll never hear the end of it."

Kyle considered this for a moment and then said, "All right. Girls can be funny sometimes." He shook his head in wonderment. "Well, I'd better go. Good luck on your acting thing."

"Thanks, Kyle. And have fun tonight. Tell the other guys I said hi."

"I will. See you, Coach."

Mark nodded and waved at the youngster as he drove off. Once Kyle was gone, Mark took one last look at the school before getting back into his truck. With a shake of his head, he exited the parking lot.

He decided to take one last loop around the Town Square. Elm street was already getting busy, and his eyes scanned the shops. He laughed as he remembered the night he saw Jenny kissing Doug and how hard that had been for him. Then he shook his head, the memories of how Cindy had baited him to go dancing with her coming to mind.

A car behind him honked and he realized he was blocking the street as he stopped in front of The Outlaws. This was his moment; why did some jerk have to ruin it? He rolled down the window to give the person a few choice words and a rude hand gesture, but then he remembered the verses Pastor Dave had spoken on Sunday.

*Love is kind.*

Mark changed his gesture to a friendly wave and proceeded forward. The person behind him gave an equally friendly wave back, making Mark smile. The single stoplight at the intersection of Elm and Mason was red and as he waited for the light to turn green. He looked once last time at the Town Square through his rear-view mirror. The misunderstandings, the trust, the holding of hands, picnics, climbing on Jenny's roof. It was all done. Now, he was on to conquer his dreams.

The light changed and he made his way out of town to the highway that would lead him down the mountains and eventually to Denver. Then it was just the matter of getting on the plane and realizing his dreams.

A half-smile played on his face as he passed the town limits and Hopes Crest disappeared behind him.

***

Denver International Airport was busy, though Mark should not have been surprised, since it was one of the most important American airports. However, somehow he had expected fewer people on the weekend. He laughed at that. Like he would know which days would be busier than others. It was not like he flew anywhere all that often.

After searching for several long minutes, Mark finally found a seat in the crowded gate lobby that faced the massive plate glass windows and sat next to a man who appeared to be in his forties with bits of gray mixed in his otherwise dark hair.

Mark gave the man a quick smile and then looked up at the numerous screens on the wall. He had at least thirty minutes before they would start boarding, so he settled himself into his seat and looked around at the people around him.

Several young children stood with their noses pressed against the glass as they watched the people in their bright orange and green vests, most with large headphones over their ears to keep out the roar of the jet engines.

The plane Mark would be boarding had not yet arrived, but a train of luggage pulled by a small cart rolled up to the plane docked at the next gate and two of the workers immediately began throwing bags into the open hatch. The children pointed and shrieked with glee as another plane rolled up to the dock on the other side, clearly enjoying the up-close and personal view of a plane in motion.

In a corner on the floor sat a teenager with earbuds in his ears as he stared at the screen on his cell phone, more than likely trying to block out the tinny sounding music that played overhead. Beside the teenager, a woman held her husband tightly, tears running down her face, and Mark sat staring at them in wonder.

"Sad," the man next to him said without looking up from his planner. "I see that all the time."

"Really?"

"Yep." He shook his head and looked up at the couple. "Some young guy out on business, going to conquer the world. The grass is always greener somewhere else and all that."

Mark scratched his head at this. "So, do you travel a lot?" he asked, glad to finally have something to do besides staring at everyone else.

"Oh, yeah. I do sales, boring stuff like shower curtains and towels, for hotels. I make good money, but it destroyed my marriage."

Mark was surprised at how matter-of-fact the man was. "How so?"

The man shrugged. "I focused on the money too much and not the relationship. She was a good woman in her own way, if you know what I mean." Mark did not miss the sad key to the man's voice and nodded, his mind immediately going to Jenny. "What about you? Where are you off to?" the man asked.

"I'm off to Hollywood," Mark explained.

The man glanced over at him, his eyebrows raised. "Is that so?"

"Yeah, I have a chance to star in a new TV series, but my girlfriend, she…well…"

"Let me guess," the man said. "She dumped you."

Mark nodded.

"Women can be funny like that," the man said with a snort. "They want everything—houses, cars, jewelry—and then get mad when you go out and get it for them. I don't think I'll ever understand them." Mark found the man's words odd; Jenny wanted none of those things. The two men talked for a while and then Mark excused himself to go to the bathroom.

When he came back several minutes later, a woman with curly, bright-red hair tapped on a microphone, causing feedback to screech through the speakers. "Sorry about that, folks," she said in a distinct southern voice. "Flight One Thirty-Two to Los Angeles will be boarding in a few minutes. I would like anyone with small children and those in business class to make their way to the boarding gate at this time."

Mark was surprised how quickly time had passed. He had not even realized the plane had already come in and its travelers had already disembarked.

It only took a few minutes before the redhead was on the mic again, calling out different sections of the plane to board, until she called out the section Mark had been assigned. "Please make your way slowly to the boarding gate at this time."

People had already begun leaping from their seats and hurriedly pushing past each other to be the first in line. One woman yelled when a man in a crisp business suit stepped on her foot, but that man did not even give her a second glance as he moved past her.

*Love is patient.*

"See you on the flight," the man sitting next to Mark said as he stood and rushed in to join the throng of people trying to find the closest spot in line they could.

Mark sat staring at the people without moving. He had time; the seats were already assigned anyway. Instead, he sat down and allowed his mind to wander. He had dreamed of becoming an actor for some time now, and now he finally had his chance. However, he also loved Jenny and dreamed about being with her.

His mind was conflicted as he wondered if he had made the wrong choice.

*Love endures all things.*

He shook his head as the scriptures flowed through his heart and mind.

*Love does not seek its own.*

Closing his eyes, he prayed for wisdom. When he was done he felt refreshed, and standing up, he grabbed hold of his suitcase. God had answered his prayers and given him his dream. Now it was time to go after it.

## *Chapter Twenty-Six*

Jenny made her way down the stairs and into the living room, Katie smiling at her with a shake to her head as a camera hung on a strap around her neck. Her once purple hair was now a bright pink.

"Oh, Jenny, you look…Wow, you are beyond beautiful," Katie said, her eyes wide.

Jenny smiled at her friend. She refused to allow Mark's leaving town to damper her plans to dress up and enjoy herself at the homecoming dance. After much deliberation, she finally had decided that she should still wear the blue prom dress and have a fun night while chaperoning the students.

"Thank you," Jenny replied as she spun around, making the skirt of the dress lift. Then a thought hit her. "You don't think it's going to be a problem wearing this, do you? I am faculty."

Katie pretended to study her closely. "It's very tasteful," she replied. "There's nothing revealing, unless sleeveless is considered too much skin."

Jenny laughed as she looked down at the dress. It had spaghetti straps and the bodice was form-fitting, but Katie was right; it was still appropriate.

"Now, if you were to wear that robe of yours tonight, then you'd be flaunting it all."

This made Jenny laugh, and she looked up just as the flash on the camera went off.

"Perfect," Katie said with a giggle. "Now, give me a pose." She took several more pictures, and Jenny moved this way and that, laughing the entire time.

When they finished, Jenny took one last look in the mirror. Her hair was curled and then swept up into a beautiful updo—Katie had insisted she go all-out on it, including adding tiny blue flowers that matched the dress. She also wore a light application of makeup, but she really did not need much, just a bit of rouge, eyeshadow, and mascara to bring out her natural coloring.

"Okay, hot stuff," Katie said, "are you ready for me to escort you to the dance?"

Jenny laughed as she grabbed her purse and then followed Katie out the door. "I told you there's no reason for you to take me," Jenny insisted for the umpteenth time. The air was chillier than she had expected, and she shivered, but having to climb back up the stairs to get her coat would be more trouble than it was worth. Plus, she would be inside where it would probably be much too warm for it, so she decided to simply deal with the cold for the time being.

"No, ma'am," Katie replied. "I'm not having my best friend driving home alone after homecoming. I'll be there to get her."

Jenny shook her head as she got into the truck. It warmed her heart that Katie was always there for her whenever she needed her. A single tear rolled down her cheek and she brushed it away, hoping Katie had not seen it.

Apparently she had. "Jenny?" Katie asked in a concerned voice. "I'm sorry. Did I do or say something wrong? You know, you can drive if you want. It's your truck after all."

Jenny smiled. "No, it's not that. It's just, the last time I went to an important dance, you had to pick me up, too." She reached into her purse and pulled out a tissue, embarrassment raging through her. "Sorry. It's just Mark. It's still too new, you know?"

Katie patted her arm and nodded before giving a heavy sigh. "I know, honey," she said and then backed the truck out into the street. "But it's okay; there are other guys out there. What about Doug? You could call him again."

Jenny loved that Katie had such an optimistic view on life. "No," Jenny replied. "I mean, I guess I could later at some point, but I think it's best to stay single for a while."

Katie nodded and thankfully changed the subject. They chatted and soon they had a bit more energy and by the time they pulled into the school parking lot, they were laughing. Jenny was not sure what she would have done without such a wonderful friend.

"Okay, a few ground rules," Katie said as she pulled up in front of gym doors. She turned and pointed her finger at Jenny, like a mother talking to her daughter. "If you meet a guy tonight, absolutely no kissing. And I want you home by midnight, not a minute later."

Jenny laughed and leaned in to give her friend a hug and a kiss on the cheek. "Love you," she said.

"I love you, too," Katie replied. "Call me whenever you're ready to leave; I'll be up all night."

"I will." Jenny got out of the truck and watched Katie drive off. She glanced around at the parking lot. In just an hour, the students would be showing up, and it would be a memorable night for them all. Her mind went to Mark and she wondered if he had made it safely to his destination. He had finally realized his dreams, though once again, he had to crush hers to get to them.

***

The cordoned-off section of the gym was packed with students and the music echoed off the walls. The night had gone well so far; there had been no fights and the students seemed to be enjoying themselves. Jenny had to only warn a few couples to watch their hands during the slow songs, but overall, everyone was respectful and appropriate. A line of students stood waiting to make requests to the DJ in the corner, and several couples danced surrounded by the remainder of the teenagers who watched, most of them clapping and singing along with the music.

Jenny was happy the students were enjoying themselves. It should be a great night for them. However, she felt a bit sorry for herself, so she went over and poured a glass of punch. One of the chaperons had informed her that it had snowed since she had arrived and that it was going to be a big storm. Jenny sighed. Of course.

She should have taken the time to run up and grab her coat after all. Oh, well, at least the truck would be warm by the time Katie picked her up.

She sipped at the fruit juice and was pleased that none of the students had tried to spike it, a feat Brett Mason had pulled her senior year. It should have gotten him expelled, but his father owned half the town, so he was only given a stern talking-to and was made to promise he would never do it again. Jenny found it all a farce, since he graduated only a few days later.

"Hey, Coach," Sam said, breaking Jenny from her thoughts. "Come dance with me." Sam looked nice in her red dress and matching red shoes and she had the biggest smile on her face.

However, the last thing Jenny wanted to do was dance. "Thanks," Jenny said, "But I'm not in the mood."

"Are you sure?" Sam insisted. "It'll be fun."

Jenny wanted to tell her no, it would not be fun. Her week had been less than wonderful, and tonight was even worse. Then a piece of scripture came to mind.

*Love is kind.*

Kindness was not always easy, Jenny realized, but it was something she usually enjoyed. So with a smile, she nodded. "Okay, just one." She set her drink down and followed Sam out to the dance floor as a song from the 1950s came on.

"Coach Jenny, I know it's none of my business," Sam shouted at her to be heard over the music, "but I'm praying for you."

"Is that so?" she asked, amused and touched at the same time.

"Yeah. I know you and Coach Mark split up. But remember, me and my mom are here if you need a friend."

Jenny nodded, and when the song ended, she gave Sam a hug. "Thank you, Sam, both you and your mom. You two are such a blessing." She glanced up and saw a boy she recognized. "Now, you better get back to Kyle before some other girl asks him to dance." She shot Sam a wink.

Sam laughed as she looked over to where Jenny nodded. "He knows better," she said and then giggled. "See you later, Coach."

Jenny smiled and walked back to the refreshment table where Kayla stood. The woman wore a full-length green gown that matched her eyes.

"You've become the talk of the town," Kayla said with a smile.

Jenny felt her stomach knot. Was the entire town talking about her and Mark's breakup? She followed Kayla's gaze over to a small group of boys, all freshmen.

"I think they're building up the courage to ask their teacher to dance."

Jenny laughed at this. "Thanks for the warning," she said and then sighed. "I guess I better get back to chaperoning. I see a boy with his hand just a bit too low on his date's back."

***

The gym now stood empty, the dance having ended an hour earlier, and everyone except Kayla and Jenny remained.

"Are you sure you have it?" Kayla asked. "I don't mind staying."

"I'm fine," Jenny replied as she moved the broom across the floor. "I'll give it a quick sweep up and come in after church tomorrow to check it over one last time. I doubt we need two people for that. The students did a great job of helping out before they left."

Kayla grabbed her coat that hung from the closed-up bleachers. "All right. I'll come with you tomorrow, though. Maybe we can grab some lunch first and then head over after we eat. How does that sound?"

Jenny smiled and gave her a nod. "Yeah, I'd like that." She gave Kayla a quick hug.

"I know you're hurting," Kayla said as the hug ended. "I won't interfere or tell you what to do, but if you haven't already, I'd recommend spending some time in prayer."

"I will, thank you," Jenny replied.

She knew Kayla was right and was grateful the woman had not tried to meddle. It was not that Jenny did not wish to share her frustrations, but at the moment, she simply wanted to be alone in her sorrow.

Maybe tomorrow she would share, but for now, she needed time to process what she was feeling on her own.

Kayla smiled and then headed out, the door banging closed behind her. Jenny caught a glimpse of the snow that was falling outside and gave a heavy sigh as she shivered just thinking about going out into the cold. The emptiness of the gym fell upon her within seconds, and though she hated to admit it, she missed Mark; missed him so much it hurt.

"I don't get it," she said, her voice echoing through the large space, "I prayed for Mark to come back, and he did. I prayed for guidance, and You gave it to me. Every step along the way, You answered my prayers, and then You took him away again? Why?"

She stood staring around her and try as she might, she could not stop the tears that fell over her lashes. She walked over and sat on a folding chair next to the bleachers and placed her head in her hands. "Lord, I try to do what's right. Mark and I both solidified our relationship with you. And then, all I wanted…"

*Love endures all things.*

Jenny felt as if the air around her had been sucked out of the room as the realization came crashing down. Yes, she did get all the things she had prayed for. Not only was her and Mark's friendship restored, so had been their love. When they grew together, however, she had not told him about her fears. No, instead, she hid that information and waited for him to mess up.

"But did he mess up?" she whispered. She bit at her lip as she pictured him tapping on the bedroom window while she held the bat, ready to swing at whoever was there. Then she thought of the dates, the prayers, and even the picnic, him supporting her and sticking up for her so they could get a new bus. He had done so much to show her he loved her; the list was endless.

Yet, when he asked her to support his dream when the opportunity had arisen once again, what did she do? She rebuked him. That was not love, that was anger, and in that anger, she had pushed him away. He had even gone so far as to be willing to wait for her, gave her time to make a decision.

She shook her head as she remembered the cheesy little display he had made. It had been so cute, and all she did was reject him. Had she truly loved him as she should have? Did she let him know her heart? No, not even close.

Guilt wracked through her as she pulled out her phone and began to type.

'I'm so sorry for what I did. You may never want to speak to me again, and I wouldn't blame you if you didn't. But just know that I am truly sorry for hurting you.'

She set the phone down on the chair and lowered herself to her knees, not caring if her dress got dirty. Closing her eyes, she offered up a prayer, "Lord, You are good in all Your ways. When my prayers were answered, I didn't respond in love. You put Mark into my life, and because I was selfish, I pushed him away. I'm sorry and ask that Mark be willing to listen to me just one more time."

When the prayer finished, she stood back up and wiped away the tears. If she was lucky, he would call her back. But if he didn't, then she would accept it and move on. Either way, she had to accept the decision God made.

She sighed heavily. It was now time to clean.

When she turned around, however, her hand went to her mouth and she gasped.

## *Chapter Twenty-Seven*

Jenny's heart raced as she looked out at the middle of the gym floor. She stifled the scream that tried to escape her lips, a scream that would have woken the entire town if she had released it. Beneath the bright lights, Mark, her one true love, stood, his face lined with exhaustion. In his hand he held a single rose.

"Mark?" Jenny asked when she was finally able to speak, still wondering if he was an illusion. Had she fallen asleep in the middle of her prayer? It would not have been the first time, although she was usually in bed when it happened. "You-you're supposed to be in California," she stammered, finding it difficult to breathe, still wondering if he really was standing there before her. "Your dream..."

"Becoming an actor had been my dream, or so I thought," he said quietly, though his voice echoed slightly, assuring her that, indeed, he was standing there. "I used to believe that it was the most important thing in my life. But, Jenny, you were the dream all along, something God showed me today."

Jenny wiped at the deluge of tears that flowed down her cheeks as she moved to stand in front of him, just as they had stood together four years earlier.

"I need to tell you something," she said, "and it's important." She waited for him to nod and then she continued. "From the first time I saw you in junior high, I've loved you. You've been the only man I could ever love since then."

He smiled down at her and said nothing, his eyes encouraging her to go on.

"You came to me a few weeks ago to tell me your dream had finally come true, that God had answered your prayers, and what did I do?"

"Jenny," he said softly as he grabbed her hands, "There's no need…"

"No, there is a need," Jenny insisted. "You see, I didn't love you all the way through. I loved you when you came back. I loved you when you did things for me, and I loved supporting you—while you were here. But when it came to the finish line, I held grudges still, I guess. I didn't even think about going with you, even though I told you I had given it some thought. That night you told me, I had already made up my mind that I wasn't going to go. Lying to someone is not how to make a relationship work."

He reached into his pocket and pulled out a tissue and handed it to her.

"Thanks," she said and she dabbed at her eyes. "If you're willing to give me another chance, I want to show you how much I love you." She swallowed hard. "Once I finish here with the volleyball season, I'm moving with you to California. I love you, Mark Davis, and I can't imagine a day without you. It's time for me to allow you to achieve your dream, and I'll be right there beside you, to support you. I have been so selfish, and though Hopes Crest will always have a special place in my heart, I need to be with the man I love."

He wiped tears from her face with his finger as he gazed down at her. "I never liked to see you cry," he said with a small smile. "And, Jenny, I love you. You have no idea how crazy I am about you. But you're not going to California."

She stared at him, confusion boring through her. "I don't understand," she said slowly. "You don't want me anymore?"

The thought that he would reject her had just now occurred to her; her selfishness once again hindering her ability to reason. Had she waited too long? Was he going to admit that he was tired of waiting for her?

"No," he said in a quiet voice, "I want you by my side forever. I thought about a lot of things while I waited at the airport for my plane to leave. I was confused, so confused. God had answered both of my prayers.

One had been that he get me a job and the other was to be with you. But as to a job, my true calling in life isn't in California, I know that now. I love acting, and I know I always will, but it was the dream of a child, of a person who did not know what love truly was. Now, though, I have learned so much, and I've found that I am supposed to be here, in Hopes Crest. I have a new dream now, or perhaps it's more like an improvement on my original dream." He put his arms around her and pulled her in. "You, and Hopes Crest."

She sobbed into him and he simply held her close, whispering words of encouragement as he kissed the top of her head.

"I love you," she said, her voice muffled by his coat.

"I love you, too," he said. When the embrace finally broke, he added, "So, Jenny, are you still my girlfriend?"

She laughed and nodded her head. "Of course," she replied. "Do you forgive me?"

"I do," he said. "And do you forgive me for taking off again like I did?"

She nodded and gave him another hug. The sadness she had felt earlier was completely gone, replaced by joy and love. "Is that for me?" she asked, indicating the rose.

"Yep," he said, holding it up in front of her. "I bought it at the gas station. It's a symbol of how precious you are to me. You're the one who supports me, stands by me. You help me through my meetings. I just want you to know that I need you more than ever in my life."

She took the flower from him and brought it to her nose. "So, I'm worth the price of a gas station rose, huh?" she asked playfully. Then she became serious again. "I love how you treat me so nicely. With every detail, you're unselfish. I need you in my life, more than you can imagine."

He glanced around the gym. "I'd love to dance with you, if you'd let me," he said. "Oh, and by the way, you look amazing in that dress. Just as amazing as you did when you wore it the first time."

She felt her cheeks burn. "You look handsome in your blazer," she said, making them both laugh. "I wish there was music."

He smiled as he pulled out his phone and pushed a few buttons.

Then he winked at her and held up a finger as he put the phone to his ear. "Okay, we're ready," he said. "Thanks again; I owe you dinner."

Jenny looked at him in confusion. "Who was that?"

He gave her a wide grin. "Kayla," he replied. "I saw her in the parking lot and we talked."

As Jenny went to speak to ask him more questions, a song began to play over the intercom. She stared up at him in shock. "That song," she gasped. "The last song we danced to."

He placed one hand around her waist and took her hand in his other. "There are no more 'last songs'," he whispered as he pulled her close.

This time there were no tears of sadness, but of joy. For love was surely all things. It was patient, it was kind, it was not selfish. Love was in forgiveness, in admitting to one another when you were stubborn. It guided one's faith and hope. And as the scriptures said, love was the greatest of them all.

***

With Mark's arm through hers, Jenny stepped outside and began to laugh. The parking lot had filled with snow, a few inches already accumulated on the ground. At first, she welcomed the cold air; their dance had certainly warmed her.

However, it did not take long before she began to shiver. She glanced down at her feet, realizing that the heels she wore would be more than uncomfortable once the wetness had made her feet cold.

"Here," Mark said, removing his blazer and helping her into it. "I swear, we need to figure out a way for you to remember your coat."

Jenny laughed as they made their way across the parking lot to Mark's truck. They took their time so she would not slip, even going so far as Mark offering to carry her.

She had adamantly declined his offer, picturing them both on the ground if he were to fall halfway across. However, she felt safe with her arm entwined with his, though her toes still became numb in no time.

Tonight had turned out to be a special night, and even cold feet could not ruin it. She was thankful for the wisdom and insight God had given her as they stopped beside Mark's truck.

"Mark," she said as she looked up at the light post next to them. "The light. It's the same one we stood under last time, when we split up."

He followed her gaze and a small frown creased his brow. But it was gone almost as soon as it appeared. "Now it's a place where we start a new path," he said as he gazed down at her. "This path is guided by the love we have for each other."

Her heart soared at his words, and a moment later, her arms were around his neck. Their lips met and Jenny could have sworn the snow around them instantly melted. There was a hunger, a passion, in that strong kiss, but most importantly, there was love.

When the kiss finally broke, she smiled up at the snow that stuck to his hair.

"Are you ready to go home?" he asked.

"I am, but give me a minute," she replied. "There's something I have to do."

She took out her phone and called Katie. Mark stared at her with a raised eyebrow but said nothing. "Katie, remember how last time you picked me up from the dance because I needed a ride home?"

"Yeah, of course I do," Katie replied. "Why? What's going on? Are you ready to be picked up?"

Jenny shot Mark a smile, her heart soaring. "Not tonight," she replied. "Tonight, Mark is taking me home."

## *Epilogue*

Jenny covered her mouth, trying her hardest not to laugh. Rehearsals for the church Christmas pageant were in full swing, and Mark stood with his eyes closed and shaking his head. She could not blame him. Mary did not understand why she had so few lines, and Joseph had the most monotone voice she had ever heard.

"Uh, Mary, should we leave before the King comes and finds us?" Joseph said and then looked at Mark, who gave a heavy sigh in response.

Jenny walked over and placed her hand on his shoulder. "Remember, 'love is patient'," she whispered in his ear.

He turned and smiled at her. "You're right," he said. "Do I ever tell you how much I love you?"

"Not today," she said with a mischievous grin.

"Well, I do."

The clearing of someone's throat made them turn, and Pastor Dave came walking up, his gaze including both of them.

"I love you guys, too," he said, "but we have a schedule to keep. Come on, director, help us out."

Everyone laughed and Jenny went back to her seat next to Kayla and watched as Mark did his magic. He spoke to the boy playing Joseph and the next time the boy spoke, he sounded much more relaxed.

Jenny realized, not for the first time, that Mark had a gift. To some he was a hometown hero for his feat on the baseball diamond and bringing home the only trophy the town of Hopes Crest had ever known.

But to Jenny, he was a hero in another way. He had battled alcoholism and its temptations and brought his life back to its fullest potential.

But even more importantly, he had shown her time and time again what love was, and she knew in her heart that their dance would go on forever.

## *Author's Note*

1 Corinthians 13:4 Love suffers long and is kind; love does not envy;
love does not parade itself, is not puffed up; 5 does not behave
rudely, does not seek its own, is not provoked, thinks no evil; 6 does
not rejoice in iniquity, but rejoices in the truth; 7 bears all things,
believes all things, hopes all things, endures all things.

1 Corinthians 13:13 And now abide faith, hope, love, these three; but the greatest of these is love.

Love. It is commanded that we love, but how many of us choose who to love and how we show that love? Loving is not always easy, especially when someone has hurt us. However, not once does the Bible teach us to love, *except when…* Jesus loved us, despite our sins, and he demonstrated that love in the greatest way possible; by giving His life in payment for those sins. Loving others is not always easy, but when we do, God's light shines through, for everything we do should glorify Him, not ourselves.

May God bless you and keep you,

Laura

# About the Author

Laura Hayes is a third-generation Coloradoan who loves God and the Rocky Mountains. She began writing Christian romance based in the fictional town of Hopes Crest, Colorado in the fall of 2018.

Her books include characters who love God, pray, go to church, and yet still make mistakes in their lives. Some are rich and some are poor; some are introverts while others are extroverts. Quite a few make wrong choices, but is that not true of us all?

However, all of her books have a message of Love, both romantic and spiritual, and the reader has the opportunity to watch both grow and develop in all her main characters.

Made in the USA
Monee, IL
18 June 2021

71638787R00113